"All this for me?" said Luton. "Why?"

"I don't know, mister, and I don't care. I just do what I'm paid to do. Frank, your horse is just over there in them bushes. Go get him so the shots don't spook him away. This won't take long."

Frank trotted across the road and into the bushes while Finney held the 10-gauge leveled at Luton's chest.

"You are going to kill me out here just like this? Not give me any idea why I'm dying? At least tell me who's paying you, if you've been paid to kill me."

"Hurry up, Frank," shouted Finney.

"Hell of a way to send a man off," said Luton.

KILLING
TIME

Robert J. Conley

BALLANTINE BOOKS • NEW YORK

Library of Congress Catalog Card Number: 88-11044

ISBN 0-345-35974-7

This edition published by arrangement with M. Evans and Company,
Inc.

Manufactured in the United States of America

First Ballantine Books Edition: May 1989

Chapter One

Sergeant Bluff Luton always sat at the same table for breakfast. He had for the last fifteen years of his life, the time he had been town marshal of Riddle, Iowa. He was about halfway through his breakfast, the same thing he always ordered, and he thought to himself that he had allowed himself to get into a rut. He drank the last of his coffee, held the cup up about eye level, and looked toward the waiter behind the bar.

"Charlie?" he said.

"More coffee, Sarge?"

"Yeah."

The front door opened and a gust of cold wind hit Luton's back. The blast was followed by a man as large as Luton and about his age. The stranger was fresh off the trail, Luton knew, because he hadn't seen him in town before. Riddle was a quiet town. Luton liked it that way. It made his job easy and, he thought, had allowed him to grow soft. But he still kept a close eye on any strangers who drifted into town. As Charlie walked over to refill his coffee cup, Luton glanced at the newcomer. He wore a parka and gloves. A scarf was tied down over his ears beneath his battered Stetson. The knee-high boots were worn but well oiled. Luton slurped his fresh, hot coffee, looking sideways at the traveler. The big man removed his Stetson and unwrapped the scarf from around his head, revealing a rugged face that needed a shave. What skin showed was red from the November cold. Luton set down his cup and picked up his fork. The stranger walked over to the bar.

"Can I get a cup of coffee in here?"

"Sure thing, mister," said Charlie, placing a cup on the counter before the man and pouring it full of steaming coffee. "That's five cents."

The man pulled off his gloves and reached into a pocket for the five-cent piece. He tossed the coin onto the bar and wrapped his big hands around the hot cup.

"It's getting cold out there," he said.

"Yeah," said Charlie. "You travel far?"

"Far enough."

The stranger took a long slurp of the hot black coffee.

"I was told down the street that I might find the marshal in here," he said.

"Right over there," said Charlie, jerking his chin toward where Luton sat.

The stranger turned with his cup in his hand and walked toward Luton. Luton put down his fork and waited until the man had stopped beside the table just across from him.

"I'm Bluff Luton," he said. "I'm the town marshal here. What can I do for you?"

"Mind if I sit down?" said the stranger.

Luton gestured toward a chair beside the man, then picked up his fork again.

"Help yourself," he said.

"My name's Finney. Tobe Finney. I'm just traveling through."

Luton continued chewing as he nodded in acknowledgment of Finney's self-introduction.

"Actually," Finney said, "there ain't nothing you can do for me. I'll be moving on directly. I just stopped in here to deliver a message for a friend."

"For me?"

"Yeah. I just come up from Texas. Wichita Falls. You know anyone down there?"

"I used to," said Luton, putting down his fork and showing interest in Finney for the first time. "It was a long time ago. Long time."

"Well, I just been there," said Finney. "Been there for a few years. Got to feeling restless. That's why I took off. When I said that I was going up this way, Will Milam asked me to stop in and see you."

"Will Milam?" said Luton. "You know Will? By God, I haven't seen Will for nigh onto twenty years. That's right. Twenty years. By God. How is he?"

"Mean as hell, I guess. He's a big man down there. Running a big cattle operation. But I didn't stop in here just to give you a howdy from an old friend."

"What then?" said Luton.

"Will said to tell you that Toad and Jasper is in Wichita County."

Luton's jaws tightened as his mind flashed back twenty years. He took a sip of coffee in an effort to force himself to relax.

"Is that all?" he said.

"That's all," said Finney, "except that Will said to tell you to be careful. 'You tell him,' he said, 'to be real careful, and tell him to look me up first.' That's what he said. 'Tell him to look me up first.' "

"Thanks, Finney," said the marshal. "Can I buy you a breakfast before you hit the trail again? A good, hot breakfast will set good on a day like this."

"Why, sure, Marshal. I don't mind."

Bluff Luton walked back to his office, unlocked the door, and stepped inside.

Damn, he thought, *I wish to hell that I had a deputy.*

Of course, he knew that there was no need for a deputy in Riddle. The town had been quiet for years. A deputy would be an added expense for the town, with no real reason for it.

Luton hadn't taken any time off for over ten years. In fact, the town council had once mentioned the possibility of hiring him some help, and he had told them that it would be a waste of good money. Now he wished that he had let them do it. Now he needed that time off. Well, he would have to think of something. He opened the gun cabinet on the wall behind his desk and took out several boxes of ammunition for his 1860 model Starr Double Action Army .44. It was one of the earliest self-cocking revolvers, and Luton was proud of it. Then he took the Winchester .44 carbine out of the cabinet and placed it beside the cartridge boxes on the desk. Stuffing the boxes in his coat pockets, he took the rifle up, stepped out of the office, and locked the door. Then he mounted his horse and rode toward his house to pack. It was going to be a long trip, and he had several loose ends to tie up in town before he could even get started.

Bluff Luton rode toward the bridge that spanned the Missouri River and connected Riddle with West Riddle, Nebraska. The wind was cold and damp. He glanced up at the sky and took note of the dark clouds which promised snow.

A hell of a time to start a trip, he thought.

He rode on across the bridge and tied his horse in front of the West Riddle marshal's office. He hadn't yet hit the ground when the door opened and a dark young man with shoulder-length hair stepped out on the sidewalk. He was wearing a black vest with a badge pinned on it.

"Hello, Blue," said Luton.

"Bluff, what brings you over here? You look like you're fixing to take a trip."

"Yeah," said Luton, "that's what brings me over here."

"Well, come on in and have a cup of coffee while you tell me about it."

The two town marshals walked inside, and the one called Blue poured two cups of coffee. They sat down at the large, cluttered desk.

"Blue," said Luton, "I'm going to Texas. You know that

I ain't got a deputy. I can't leave my town without some protection."

"Texas?" said Blue. "That's a long trip, especially in this kind of weather. It's going to get worse, too. Snow pretty soon."

"Damn, I know it. I've got to go, and I've got to go now."

"What is it, Bluff?"

"I'm going after two men."

"Bluff, you got no jurisdiction down there."

"This is personal," said Luton.

"You want to tell me about it?"

"No," said Luton. "I just want you to trust me."

"You want me to ride with you?"

"No, but I do need your help. I want to make you my deputy. I need you to stay here while I'm gone."

"That would give me two towns to watch—in two different states. Is that legal?"

"Hell, I don't know if it's legal or not, Blue, but I know that you can take care of it, and I know that we can get both our town councils to go along with it if we ask them. Will you do it?"

Blue Steele looked at Luton. He had never seen the man look so grim. Whatever it was that he wanted these two men for, it must be important, he thought. He remembered how Luton had helped him out in his time of need and how, in fact, Luton had helped put him in his present position of town marshal.

"Sure, Bluff," he said. "I'll do it."

As Sergeant Bluff Luton turned his mount back toward the Missouri River bridge to recross into Iowa, he saw the first snowflakes fall. He looked up into the sky and felt them hit his face.

"Damn," he said. "At least I'll be heading south."

The southbound stagecoach pulled into Riddle a few minutes late, and an impatient Bluff Luton threw his blanket roll and a small valise up on top. He had been to see Mayor Miller and arranged for Blue Steele, the town marshal across the river, to serve as deputy for Riddle in his absence, assuming that Steele would do the same on his end. He didn't know how long he would be gone, he had told Miller. What was the purpose of his trip? Personal business. He would take a leave of unspecified duration with no pay. Luton's salary was small, and his savings were, therefore, meager. He withdrew every penny he had in the bank and stuffed the money into his pockets.

"Going somewhere, Sarge?" said the driver of the stage as he groaned, climbing down from the box.

"Texas, Elmer," said Luton.

"Well, keep your pants on. I'm going to be a few minutes here."

"I know."

Of course he knew. He had watched the business of the stage for fifteen years in Riddle. Didn't Elmer know that? Damn, he thought. He realized that his irritation was simply a result of his impatience—his desire to get this trip under way. It was going to be a long and tedious journey with nothing to do along the way but think. He wasn't looking forward to that. Elmer stepped up on the sidewalk beside Luton.

"I can't take you all the way to Texas, Sarge. You know that, don't you?"

"Damn it, Elmer," said Luton. "I know your goddamned route better than you do. Just get on with your business so we can get the hell out of here."

"All right. All right. You don't need to bite my head off."

Elmer trudged off grumbling to himself, leaving Luton to pace the boards of the sidewalk. It seemed to Luton that Elmer took twice as long as usual for his Riddle stop. At long last Elmer was ready to roll, and Luton was inside the coach with three other passengers. Two ladies were facing forward, one middle-aged and protective of the other, a young lady probably not yet twenty. They talked of visiting relatives in

Omaha. Across from the ladies sat Luton next to a man of
about thirty wearing a business suit. Luton breathed a sigh
of relief when the stage lurched forward. He would be glad
to get this first leg of the trip over. At Omaha he would catch
another stage going to St. Joseph, Missouri. He could catch
a train at Omaha, but he would have to ride it clear to Denver,
Colorado, before he could get one heading south. At St. Jo,
he could catch trains going almost directly toward his destination. The lines had only recently been connected through
the Indian Territory and on down into Texas. He would wind
up at a small town called Henrietta, and from there he would
have to take a stage again to travel the last eighteen miles
into Wichita Falls.

Luton thought about Wichita Falls. He had been there
some twenty years earlier. There hadn't seemed to him to be
enough of it to deserve a name then. He figured it had grown
some since those days. He didn't know how much. He wondered what the place was like twenty years later, and he
wondered how Will Milam was doing. That stranger—what
was his name? Finney. Finney had said that Will was a big
cattleman. Luton hoped so. Will deserved it. *A big cattleman*, he thought. *Well, I guess I'd be a big cattleman, too,
instead of riding in this stage carrying every cent I own to
my name, if I'd stayed with Will instead of running out on
him like I done. I guess. Well, what the hell?*

Will Milam had been a good friend, and the time might
have been pleasant to remember had not the thought of Will
and Luton's days with him brought along with it other, less
pleasant memories. Luton did not want to think about those
things—not yet. It was going to be a long trip. He settled
back into the seat and tried to force the thoughts out of his
mind. If he could make himself sleep, it might help.

Luton slept. He slept, but he had been wrong about the
effect of the sleep. It didn't help. His sleep was fitful and
troubled by visions of a face he did not want to see. It was
the face of a handsome young man—really just a boy—a boy

trying to be a man. The face smiled. It was full of life and promise. It laughed a youthful, innocent laugh. Then there was a pistol. It was an old 1851 model Navy Colt .36. A thumb pulled back the hammer, and a dirty finger squeezed the trigger. The blast jarred Luton out of his sleep. He was sweating in the cold November air, and he could hear Elmer up above calling out to the horses.

"Whoa. Whoa up there."

Elmer was stopping the coach. Luton was sure that he couldn't have slept that long. Where were they? What was going on? Then a strange voice came from outside.

"Raise your hands up high, mister."

Luton reached for his Starr revolver, but before he could get it out of the holster, he felt a barrel poke into his side.

"Just sit still, Marshal."

The man in the business suit had him covered. Luton figured out the situation in an instant. The passenger was obviously an accomplice to the robber outside. *Damn*, he thought. *What a hell of a stupid situation for me to get caught in.* The years at Riddle had made him soft. He eased his hand away from the Starr and leaned back into the seat again. The older lady was clutching the younger one tightly to her bosom.

"Just relax, ladies," said the man with the gun. "Nothing's going to happen to you. You have my word."

"Frank," came the voice from outside. "You in there?"

Luton thought that the voice sounded vaguely familiar, but he couldn't quite place it.

"I'm in here," said the man with the gun.

"You got him?"

"I got him."

"Come on out."

"Okay, Marshal," said Frank. "Step outside and keep your hands away from that gun."

Luton opened the stage door and stepped out onto the ground. The snow was beginning to stick, and a cold wind blew across the river. He had slept longer than he thought, for he could see the wooded hills lining the road off to the east. The man called Frank stepped out of the coach behind him and gave him an easy shove away from the door. Luton looked up to see Tobe Finney astride a rangy mustang, holding a Remington 10-gauge shotgun. Finney had both Luton and Elmer within eyesight and range.

"Mr. Finney," said Luton, "I didn't expect to see you out here."

"No, I suppose not," said Finney. "Driver, throw down your shotgun, real careful."

Elmer did as he was told.

"Now your belt gun," said Finney.

Elmer picked the pistol out of his belt gingerly between thumb and forefinger and tossed it.

"That's real good," said Finney. "Now you can just whip up them horses and be on your way."

Elmer hesitated an instant, probably out of surprise, then lashed at his team, taking the stage on its way. Finney held the shotgun on Luton while Frank watched the stagecoach get smaller and smaller.

"All this for me?" said Luton. "Why?"

"I don't know, mister, and I don't care. I just do what I'm paid to do. Frank, your horse is just over there in them bushes. Go get him so the shots don't spook him away. This won't take long."

Frank trotted across the road and into the bushes while Finney held the 10-gauge leveled at Luton's chest.

"You going to kill me out here just like this? Not give me any idea why I'm dying? At least tell me who's paying you, if you've been paid to kill me."

"Hurry up, Frank," shouted Finney.

"Hell of a way to send a man off," said Luton.

The bushes rustled and a sorrel mare appeared. Its rider was barely visible from where Finney and Luton waited. He was blocked from their vision by the horse. The animal moved at an angle perpendicular to her presumed destination.

"Come on, Frank," said Finney, his voice betraying his impatience.

"Hey."

That last came from the man behind the horse. Finney looked and saw a rifle laid across the saddle and aimed directly at him. He squinted toward the man, but he couldn't see him well. It wasn't Frank. He swung the shotgun around, but before he could fire, the rifle jerked up from the saddle on which it rested. The sound of its shot echoed back from the far hillsides, and a .44-.40 slug tore through Finney's left clavicle, knocking him backward out of the saddle. The man stepped out from behind the sorrel and started walking toward Luton.

"Blue Steele," said Luton. "What the hell are you doing here? Not that I ain't glad to see you."

Steele walked on over to Luton, leading the sorrel.

"Your trip's barely started and you're already in trouble, Sarge," he said. "I don't know if I should let you go on by yourself."

"Blue," said Luton, "there's another one."

"Oh," said Blue, "the guy that belongs to this horse? I cut his throat back there in the bushes."

"But what the hell are you doing here?"

"That Finney feller came into West Riddle bragging about how he set you up and telling what he was going to do to you. I guess he'd had a little too much to drink, and the last time he'd been up this way, West Riddle was a wide open town. He didn't know that things have changed over there. I guess he also thought that he was pretty safe talking to a long-haired half-breed. Anyhow, I let him ride out. The coach was already gone. And I followed him. That's all."

"Blue, I sure do thank you. I'm in your debt again."

"Never mind about that. The important thing is that Finney was hired by two men down in Texas. The two men that you're going after, I expect. That means they know you're coming and they're laying for you. Finney might not be the only one you meet up with along the way. Keep your eyes open, buddy.''

"I will after this," said Luton.

"Well," said Blue, "grab that mustang, and I'll ride this sorrel. Let's catch that stagecoach and get you back on it. Then I'll turn around and clean up this mess."

Chapter Two

Bluff Luton sat on a hard, straight bench in the office of the stage lines in Omaha, Nebraska, waiting for the connecting stage to take him on down to St. Joseph, Missouri. He had a two-hour wait. That gave him just what he didn't want—time to think. What was more, he had something else to think about after the episode on the trail with Finney. What had Blue Steele said? ". . . they know you're coming . . ." That changed things considerably. He had started this trip thinking that he was the hunter, that he would have the element of surprise on his side. He had received a message from his old friend and partner, Will Milam, that Toad and Jasper were in Wichita County. He had no reason to expect that the two men knew that he had received the message. But the messenger had tried to kill him—had even boasted in West Riddle about how he had set him up for the kill. Blue Steele's quick assessment of the situation was the only one that made any sense: the message had been a lie. It had come, not from Will Milam, but from Toad and Jasper themselves. Toad and Jasper were the hunters. They were after him. It was funny. He had not known, had never suspected, that they wanted to kill him as badly as he wanted to kill them.

Blue Steele had also intimated that Finney and his name-

less partner might not be the only ones along the long trail
to Texas waiting to ambush Luton. Luton realized that he
was edgy. He was keeping his right hand free and his coat
pushed back behind the Starr revolver which hung at his right
side. He was watching with a nervous eye every man who
came into the stage office, and he had very carefully placed
himself in the room where no one could walk up behind him.
It was going to be a very different kind of trip from what he
had thought it would be.

Goddamn those two, he thought. Goddamn Toad and Jasper all the way to hell.

He could see their faces leering. He ached to wipe the ugly
leers away once and for all. He could see them . . . But he
forced the images out of his mind. The trip was going to be
too long. He did not want to remember. Not now. Not yet.
He looked around the room at the men who, with him, waited
for the southbound stage. He searched their faces for any hint
of something suspicious, some reason to be wary of this one
or that one, but he knew that he was really just trying to get
his mind on something in the present. Better to concentrate
on present danger than to recall the unpleasant past. He could
find no one in the room to be particularly distrustful of. Yet,
he thought, how would one distinguish a hired killer? The
passenger in the business suit on the stage into Omaha who
had turned out to be Finney's partner had seemed innocent
enough.

The two hours passed without incident, and the passengers
were loaded onto the stage. With a sudden lurch, they were
on the way to St. Jo. Already, Luton noted, it was no longer
snowing. At least that was good. He decided that he would
not sleep on this trip. He would try to stay awake. It would
be a long and boring ride, and awake, he would have trouble
keeping his mind from wandering back into the past. He tried
to accomplish both purposes—the staying awake and the not
thinking of the past—by studying the landscape. He watched
for likely ambush spots. He took note of the topographical
changes as the coach moved steadily southward. The coun-

tryside grew more hilly, and the trees were more abundant. Luton wondered if he would know when they crossed into Missouri by the lay of the land or by instinct or from his memory. When it happened, he knew because the driver shouted out from his seat up topside, "Crossing into Missouri, folks." Having crossed the Missouri River twice and ridden seemingly endless hours in the pitching, lurching, tossing stagecoach, he felt by crossing into Missouri his journey had finally gotten under way. But Missouri in his mind was outlaw country. His fancy told him that Toad and Jasper would likely have more men lined up and waiting for him in Missouri. He tried to force himself to be more alert, but simply became drowsy and once again fell asleep. Later, when the driver pulled back on the reins and shouted, "Whoa," and stopped the coach, which rocked violently back and forth before settling down, Luton came awake with a start and reached for his revolver. The passenger sitting directly across from him, a railroad official traveling on business from Omaha to St. Joseph, jerked his hands up in fright.

"Hey," he said, "what is this?"

"Why are we stopping?" said Luton, looking out the window.

"Get out and stretch your legs, folks," came the voice of the driver. "Just a little rest stop."

Luton took his hand away from his gun and felt his face burning with embarrassment.

"I'm sorry," he said. "I'm just a little edgy, I guess. I was asleep. I'm sorry."

He climbed cautiously out of the coach and walked around, stretching his limbs and sucking in the crisp Missouri air. He walked all around the coach several times, and as he did so, trying to appear casual, he took note of their surroundings and saw nothing suspicious. As far as he could tell, he and his fellow travelers were the only human beings within miles. He relaxed a little, and the rest of the ride on into St. Jo was uneventful.

* * *

Walking through the busy streets of St. Jo, Luton tried to keep to the walls as much as possible. He carried the valise in his left hand, the blanket roll under his left arm. That way he kept his right free. He watched the people around him warily, and he thought about Will Milam. Since the message he had received through Finney had come from Toad and Jasper themselves, this meant that Milam was not even aware of the fact that Luton was on his way to Texas. In fact, Luton realized, Milam might not even be in Wichita County anymore. It had been years since Luton and Milam had seen each other, and they had not even tried to keep in touch. The message had been sent to him as if it had come from Milam, but that had probably been done only so that Luton would respond to it by making the trip without any suspicion. Toad and Jasper would know that Luton wanted them badly enough to go after them, and they would also know that Luton would trust Will Milam. Well, there was nothing to do about it but to continue on the journey. Continue on the journey and stay alert. Anything could happen.

Hurrying down the street, a big man with the look and smell of a buffalo hunter bumped into Luton and sent him spinning. Luton's Starr revolver was out and leveled at the man in an instant. The buffalo hunter's hands went up.

"Whoa, there," he said. "Hold on now, mister. I shoulda been watching where I was going. I own it. Ain't no call to shoot a man."

Luton felt foolish. People were staring, waiting eagerly in hopes of witnessing a slaughter. The man had, after all, probably just accidentally bumped into him. It was a crowded street, and the crowd was growing thicker the closer he got to the railroad depot. On the other hand, the big man might have been one of Toad and Jasper's hired assassins. Luton kept the Starr leveled at the hunter's belly.

"Okay," he said. "Just go on then. Go on."

The hunter hurried on down the street, and Luton waited until he was nearly out of sight before he reholstered the Starr. A young man in knickers stood gawking.

"What the hell's the matter with you?" said Luton. "Disappointed you didn't see someone killed? Get out of here."

The kid turned and ran. Luton once more felt the Starr at his hip, looked around at the crowd, shifted the weight of the blanket roll he carried under his left arm, and started walking again toward the depot.

Jumpy, he thought. *I'm too damn jumpy.*

At the depot he had to stand in line for a ticket, and he discovered that he had a considerable wait in St. Jo before the southbound train's departure. He decided that a drink might calm his nerves, so, concealing his valise in his blanket roll and entrusting both to the station manager, he went out to look for a saloon. The nearest one was just a couple of blocks down the street. It was crowded, but Luton went inside. He edged his way through the mass of customers and found a place at the bar where he ordered a shot of rye whiskey. He had acquired a taste for the stuff when drinking with Blue Steele. The bartender poured the drink, and Luton paid for it, picked it up in his left hand, and turned to lean on the bar facing out at the crowd. As he sipped the whiskey, he looked over the faces he could see there before him. He was amazed to discover that they all looked like hired killers. He finished the drink and made his way back out of the saloon and onto the street. An alleyway provided a shorter route back to the depot, and Luton turned down it. He hadn't taken more than a half dozen steps when two men stepped out of a shadowed doorway and stood before him. One held a club in his hand, the other a knife. They stared at him but didn't speak. Luton stopped. The two men shot quick glances at each other and fidgeted in their tracks. Luton moved to one side of the alley as if to walk past the men, and they shuffled across the alley to block his path.

"Get the hell out of my way," said Luton.

"Now," said the man with the club, and he took a wild swing just as Luton reached for his Starr. The club missed, but the man's arm blocked Luton's attempt to draw his weapon. The man with the knife was moving in. Luton

grabbed the other in a bear hug and swung him around to
block the knife. As the would-be knifer circled, trying to get
into a position where he could lunge at Luton, Luton turned
in a circle, keeping the other man between them. Luton's
bear hug was powerful, and its victim found his arms useless.
He flailed them around in the air harmlessly. This could go
on all day, thought Luton. He suddenly released his grip and
shoved the man with the club into the other one. As they
scrambled to regain their balance, Luton jerked the Starr out
of its holster and leveled it at them.

"Stop right there," he said.

The slasher made a quick move with his knife toward
Luton, and Luton fired. The bullet tore into the man's upraised
arm between the biceps and the triceps, smashing the bone.
The arm fell limp and bloody at the man's side. His knife
dropped to the dirt. The man screamed in horror. His partner
dropped his club to the ground and raised his hands above
his head.

"Don't shoot," he said. "Don't shoot. We quit."

"I need a doctor," said the wounded man. "Get me a
doctor."

"You two are going to walk ahead of me to the nearest
law officer," said Luton. "I don't know this city. Sheriff's
office? Town marshal? Police chief? You lead the way."

"Let's just forget it, huh?" said the man who had dropped
the club. "Let us go. We won't bother you again."

"I need a doctor."

"You two don't lead me to a jailhouse," said Luton, looking at the healthy one, "I'll shoot you, too, and leave you
both here to bleed to death. Get moving."

As the two attackers started slowly down the alley, Luton
picked up the knife and the club in his left hand, keeping the
Starr in his right pointed at their backs and followed them.
Moving back out onto the sidewalk, Luton felt himself for
the second time to be the center of a spectacle in St. Jo. The
wounded man left a gory trail as he whimpered his way toward the jail.

* * *

"Howdy," said Luton, still puffing from the excitement and the exertion of the fight in the alley. "I've got a couple of would be assassins here."

Luton closed the door behind himself as the sheriff stood up behind his desk.

"What's happened?" said the sheriff.

"Sheriff," said Luton, holstering his Starr, "I'm Bluff Luton. I'm town marshal of Riddle, Iowa. I'm on my way down to Texas on personal business, and I have reason to believe that there are persons who do not want me to finish my trip. The stagecoach out of Riddle was held up by two hired killers for the sole purpose of murdering me. And now these two have attacked me in an alley down by the railroad depot."

He tossed the club and the knife onto the sheriff's desk.

"Here are their weapons."

"I need a doctor," whimpered the wounded man.

"We ain't no hired killers," said the other.

"Both of you shut up and get into the cell," said the sheriff.

"I'm bleeding," said the whiner.

"You'll get a doctor. Inside."

The sheriff locked the cell door, excused himself to Luton, and stepped out onto the sidewalk, where he found someone to send for the doctor. Then he stepped back inside. He poured two cups of coffee and offered one to Luton, who accepted. Then he sat back down behind his desk.

"Mr. Luton," he said, "I've heard about you. Thanks for corralling those two and bringing them down here, by the way."

He took a sip of his hot coffee.

"Wasn't nothing else I could do," said Luton.

"Well," continued the sheriff, "I hate to argue with your theory, but I don't think that these two were hired to kill you. I know them. They've been hanging around St. Jo for some time. I've suspected them of several beatings and robberies, but I've never been able to prove anything on them until now. Since you've already had one other attempt made on your life on this trip and seem to expect more, it may be difficult for you to accept this as a weird coincidence, but that's just exactly what I believe it is.''

"The one man came at me with a knife," said Luton.

"I believe you," said the sheriff, "and I'll charge him with attempted murder and robbery. I'm just saying that I don't think there's any connection here between this incident and the other one you told me about.''

Luton shoved the hat back on his head and scratched at his scalp.

"Maybe you're right," he said. "This whole thing's got me kind of jumpy, I guess. If you know these two, then you're probably right.''

He pulled the watch out of his pocket and studied it.

"Listen," he said, "if you need some kind of statement from me or anything like that, could we get on with it? I've got a train to catch.''

Chapter Three

Bluff Luton was on the ground. The pain from the bullet wound in his chest was intense and he felt like all his strength had drained out of him through the bullet hole. The world around him seemed hazy, as if he were looking at it through a fog, but even through the fog, he could see Bud leaning over him. He could read panic and fear and concern on his young and handsome face. And he himself felt helpless. It was he who should be protecting Bud, not the other way around, and here he was lying helpless on the ground and Bud bending over him. The world seemed upside down. He tried to get up. He couldn't move. He tried to say something. He couldn't speak. All of this had transpired in only a few seconds, and Bud had stood up to face the attackers. Then Bluff Luton had seen the dirty hands raise the sawed-off 12-gauge shotgun. He tried again to heave himself up off the ground, to scream, but he couldn't move. He heard the laughter, evil and ugly. He saw the face behind the gun, the leering face of Toad Jessup. He saw the finger squeeze the trigger, and he heard the indescribably loud blast of the shotgun. He screamed, or he thought that he screamed, but the only sound was the blast of the shot and its echo. The

young man had been thrown backward in a shower of blood.
Then the gun had been aimed at Bluff.

"Save your shot," he had heard Jasper say. "He's dy-
ing."

Then he had seen the big boot of Jasper Jessup coming
toward him, and then everything went black.

Luton awoke in a sweat. It was cold in the passenger car,
yet he was sweating. The images remained vivid in his head.
They were images that he had lived with day and night for a
good many years, but he had finally, he thought, managed
to put them to rest. Not so. The news of the whereabouts of
the Jessups, Toad and Jasper, the fact that he was traveling
to find them, the implication that they were, in all probabil-
ity, laying an ambush for him, all these things had brought
the awful images back to the forefront of his mind. Even
though he was involved in a journey of six or seven hundred
miles or more in pursuit of revenge, he did not want to think
about the thing that drove him to it. He did not want to
remember coming slowly to consciousness, feeling more
dead than alive. His mind rebelled against the recollection
of crawling, slowly and painfully, through the north Texas
dirt to the awful spectacle of the body which had so lately
housed his younger brother, Bud. He did not want to feel
once again the overwhelming sense of guilt at having failed
in his responsibility to protect, to nurture, to care for, to look
out for his teenaged charge.

Luton shook his head in a futile effort to shake out the
memories, and he looked out of the window at the Missouri
landscape racing by. He wondered how long it would be
before the railroad made it all the way into Riddle. Soon,
probably, he thought. This is the future. This is the way to
travel, all right. How the hell could road agents stop one of
these things anyhow? He decided that he was going to keep
his mind busy with anything in order to keep it from wandering back to the past. He could study the railroad car, and
when he had done that, he could get up and walk around to
see more of the train. He could speculate about the future of

travel in this country. He wondered how much Texas had
changed since he had last seen it. He could spend some time
speculating on that. He could study the changing landscape
as he traveled farther south, and the changing climate. Already, he noticed, it was getting warmer, and it was no longer
snowing. He wondered if the snow was piling up back in
Riddle. He could even think about Toad and Jasper and what
he would do to them when he cornered them, if they didn't
get him first. He could think about that, but that was as close
as he wanted to get to thinking about the past. That last
thought brought back to mind for Luton what, he decided,
should be his main concern. The first order of business was
getting to the end of the line alive. If they should get to him
first, then none of it mattered anyhow.

What the hell's wrong with me? he asked himself. *I've
gone soft. Too many years in Riddle. Soft job. No problems.*

He thought about how he had been puffing and blowing
after the fight with the two hoodlums in St. Jo. *Out of shape.
Gone soft. Getting old, Damn it.* The train ride wasn't helping any either. *A damn soft way to travel*, he thought. But
the train ride was necessary. It was a long enough trip even
with the railroad, and there was no guarantee that the Jessups
would still be in Wichita County when he got there. He was
in a hurry. But *if they want me as bad as I want them, they
will be there. There or somewhere along the way.* He looked
furtively around the passenger car at his fellow travelers. All
looked suspicious to Luton. He thought again about the fight
in St. Jo. The sheriff had said that it was just a coincidence,
that those two were small-time, local thugs. They had just
been attempting to rob him. But Luton wasn't sure of that.
So what if they were known local riffraff? The Jessups, or
some agent of theirs, could have paid them a dollar or two
and pointed him out to them. Such things had happened
before.

He stood up and stepped out into the aisle to stretch himself. A walk might help. He staggered because of the movement of the train as he made his way toward the rear of the

car. He thought that it was peculiar for him to be walking
one direction while traveling rapidly in the opposite direction. The train lurched around a curve, and Luton fell to one
side. He caught himself on the back of a seat and regained
his balance, but in the process he jostled the passenger sitting
there.

"Excuse me," he said.

The offended passenger looked up at Luton from under the
flat brim of a Montana peak hat. Luton noticed the hat because it was banded with a rattlesnake skin, the rattles dangling off to one side. The man was medium-sized, but
rawboned and hard looking, perhaps a few years younger
than Luton. He wore no jacket, but he had on a heavy, dark
wool shirt, buttoned all the way up to the collar, and he wore
a tie with a pearl stickpin that looked as if it belonged with
a business suit. Light-colored corduroy trousers were tucked
into the tops of a pair of high-topped, fancy, mule-eared
boots. He wore a six-gun strapped high on his waist, more
in front than on his side. The holster was attached to the
same belt that ran through the belt loops of his trousers.
Luton took all this in instantly, partly because of his in-
creased vigilance and partly because of the incongruity of
the man's appearance. He touched the brim of his hat to add
an appropriate physical gesture to his verbal apology. The
man was staring at him.

"Never mind," said the man.

There was nothing particularly noticeable about the man's
features aside from small, steely gray eyes and a bushy,
sandy-colored mustache which obliterated the shape of his
mouth. Luton moved on. Funny, he thought, that he should
bump into that particular passenger, the most suspicious
looking one in the car. The man was no cowboy. Luton was
sure of that, in spite of the fancy cowboy boots. The tie was
wrong. A cowboy would wear a bandanna. The fancy boots
were not beat up—showed no scuff marks. And the man was
too old, he thought. He had the look of a killer. Then Luton
caught himself. He was being ridiculous. What does a killer

look like? What, for that matter, does a cowboy look like?
He was, he realized again, too jumpy, too suspicious of anyone and everyone. Still, he would watch the man, along with
everyone else around him. He would maintain his vigilance.
He had, after all, been twice attacked already on this trip.
The job at Riddle had made him soft—not just physically but
mentally. He had been able, he realized, to relax much too
much. This new situation and recent events had forced him
to the other extreme. He had to find a proper balance between
the two.

He strolled through two passenger cars, then reversed himself and went back to his seat. As he sat down, he caught the
eye of the man he had jostled just a few minutes earlier. The
man quickly turned his eyes away, but Luton was certain that
the man had been watching him. He wondered what kind of
pistol was jammed into the high holster on the man's waist.
He hadn't had time to get a good look at that. You could tell
a lot about a man by the kind of sidearm he carried, Luton
thought. The man rolled a cigarette and lit it, making Luton
want to smoke, but there were ladies sitting near him in the
car. That didn't stop some of the male passengers, but it
stopped Luton. He tried to keep his eyes off the smoker, but
he found that they kept roving back in that direction.

After a frustrating side trip east to Macon, Missouri, then
southeast on the Northern Missouri Railroad, Luton connected with the Pacific Railroad of Missouri heading west to
Kansas City. He would not go all the way to Kansas City but
would get off at Sedalia, where he could catch a ride on the
newly completed Missouri, Kansas and Texas line, which
would take him the rest of the way on his journey. The M.,
K. and T., or Katy, as it was being called, would take him
first of all through Fort Scott, Parsons, and Chetopa, Kansas,
then through the Indian Territory and on into Texas. Luton
wondered what would happen at Sedalia. Which passengers
would continue on to Kansas City and which ones would join
him on the Katy? Would the smoker, the man he had jostled,
be on the Katy? If he was one of the Jessups' hired killers,

he certainly would follow Luton onto the Katy—unless he tried something before they got that far.

At Sedalia, Luton got off the train. Nothing had happened. The man with the high-hung pistol had gotten off ahead of Luton and walked on down the street without looking back. He didn't seem to be in the least interested in keeping track of Luton. Most of the passengers rushed off the cars and headed straight for the station house. Those who were going on to Kansas City had ten minutes in which to grab something to eat and get back on the train. Luton was not in such a hurry. The Katy, heading south, would not leave for two more hours. He decided to take his time and avoid the crowd, and he let them all rush ahead of him into the station. He strolled on up to the doorway of the station and looked inside.

Luton thought it looked like a madhouse in there. All the passengers seemed to be shouting at once, trying to get a bite to eat or a cup of coffee from the half dozen or so waiters behind the counter before their ten allotted minutes expired. Luton watched as people pushed one another to get a spot at the counter. He saw one man bump another, spilling the victim's coffee onto his chest and stomach. People seemed to be rushing back and forth with no particular destination in mind. At any other time, Luton would have found it all very amusing, but he wasn't in a mood for humor. A man rushed out the door right past Luton. He had a bag in each hand and a large biscuit clutched in his teeth. So far as Luton could tell, no one was at all interested in his whereabouts. High Holster had vanished. Soon a conductor, standing calmly in a doorway opposite where Luton stood, held out before him a large railroad watch. He called out for boarding to the Kansas City passengers and stepped deftly aside to avoid the mad rush that his call precipitated. Only a few passengers remained at the counter. Luton walked to an end of the counter next to a wall. He tossed his blanket roll and

valise down on one stool and sat on another. A waiter turned
toward him.

"I'll try a cup of that 'Celebrated Sultana Coffee,' " said
Luton, reading from the lettering on one of the large urns
behind the counter.

As the waiter walked a few steps away and reached under
the counter, a voice came from over Luton's shoulder.

"Get a clean cup," it said, "and let me see you fill it out
of that urn."

The waiter, bending from the waist, looked up into the
face the voice had come from. Luton turned and looked over
his shoulder. There was High Holster, staring at the waiter
with his steely eyes. The waiter moved back to a stack of
clean cups piled beside the urn.

"Get two of them," said High Holster. Then he sat down
at the stool next to Luton's blanket roll.

"You eating?" he said.

Luton eyed the man with a burning curiosity.

"Yeah," he said.

"Better have the beefsteak and eggs. The stew's prairie
dog."

The waiter brought the two cups of fresh coffee, and High
Holster reached across the counter and caught him by his
white necktie.

"Bring two orders of steak and eggs," he said. "Bring
fresh. If you bring anyone's leftovers, you won't last the
night."

"Yes sir," said the waiter. "It'll be fresh. I guarantee it."

The man released his grip, and the waiter vanished into
the kitchen.

"What kind of show is this?" said Luton.

"Ah, these whistle-stops are all alike," said the stranger.
"They rush folks through so fast that half of them don't finish
what they ordered. Then the waiters take it back behind the
counter and sell it over again to the next sucker who orders
the same thing."

"Who are you?"

"Name's Oliver Colfax."

"I've heard of you, Colfax," said Luton. "I'm—"

"I know who you are," said Colfax, interrupting Luton's introduction. "What've you heard?"

"I've heard that you earn your living with that revolver you're wearing up there on your waistline, and I've heard that you're wanted for murder in Arizona."

"You heard right. Both times. How's your coffee?"

"Not bad," said Luton. "Never had any of this 'Celebrated Sultana' before."

He noticed that the pistol in the high holster was a Colt .45—a Peacemaker. The waiter came back with two plates and placed one in front of each of the two men.

"More coffee?" he asked.

Colfax nodded, and Luton shoved his cup toward the waiter. The waiter took both cups back to the urn, refilled them, then brought them back to the counter and took himself as far away from his two customers as he was able. Luton cut into his steak.

"I haven't heard any rumors lately," he said. "Where've you been?"

"Texas."

"What part?"

"Sherman. Denison. Wichita Falls."

"It's been a long time since I've been down that way," said Luton. "Railroad go into Wichita Falls yet?"

"Not yet. There's talk."

"How's the cattle business down that way?"

"Thriving. How's your steak?"

"Good. It's good."

"Eggs cooked all right?"

"Just right."

"Good."

Luton waved his coffee cup in the air at the waiter, who hurried back to refill both cups, then quickly retreated again.

"Where you headed, Colfax?" asked Luton.

"Texas."

"Wichita Falls?"

"Yeah."

Neither man spoke again until they had finished their meal. Then Luton stood up and reached into his pocket.

"I'm paying," said Colfax.

Luton stood still and watched while Colfax called the waiter back over and paid for both meals. He picked up his blanket roll and tossed it over his shoulder, then picked up the valise in his left hand. Colfax turned as if he were going to walk out of the station without saying another word, but Luton stopped him with a question.

"Colfax," he said, "to what do I owe all this?"

Colfax stopped and looked over his shoulder at Luton.

"It's the least I could do," he said.

"For what?"

"Don't you know?"

Luton didn't bother answering that query. He stared at Colfax for a few seconds until Colfax decided to finish the discussion. The man with the Peacemaker high on his hip turned to face Luton. He looked him straight in the eyes.

"I'm going to kill you," he said.

Chapter Four

Sergeant Bluff Luton had just settled down in his seat in the passenger car of the southbound Katy train. He saw a few passengers in the car he recognized from the previous train, but most of them were new faces. He hadn't seen Colfax since the man had left him in the station house. The car wasn't crowded. No one sat on the bench next to Luton, nor on the one he was facing. He tossed his blanket roll and valise onto the seat beside him. Where is that damn Colfax? he wondered. Why did he give himself away like that? Some kind of perverse pride maybe. Luton had heard that Oliver Colfax was a strange man. Now he had firsthand evidence to that effect. But why was the man not on the train, and when would he strike? When and how? Of course, Luton realized, Colfax might be on the train. Just because he had not seen the man board and didn't find him on the same passenger car, that didn't mean that he hadn't boarded and wasn't in another car. Colfax was a slick one.

The door at the end of the car behind Luton's back opened suddenly, increasing the noise of the track and the wheels. It shut again. Luton looked over his shoulder. It was Colfax. Luton's right hand automatically went for the Starr at his side, but before he could pull it out of its holster, Colfax raised both his hands up in front of his chest, holding them palms toward Luton, fingers spread. Luton sat still. Colfax moved to the bench across from Luton.

"Do you mind?" he said.

"Be my guest," said Luton. "I'd rather have you there than behind me."

"You don't have to watch your back, Luton. Not on my account. I don't work that way."

"When, Colfax?"

"I'll let you know."

Luton suddenly, unexpectedly, relaxed. He believed this man. It was a strange feeling to be sitting casually across from a man who had announced his intention to kill him. Colfax rolled himself a cigarette and offered Luton the makings. Luton looked around. He decided that he was a proper distance from any ladies in the car, so he accepted. The smoke tasted good. It felt good to be relaxed again. Maybe relaxed wasn't the right word, but he wasn't edgy and jumpy the way he had been. He knew his adversary, and he knew that he would receive some kind of warning before imminent danger. He looked through the smoke at Colfax.

"I think I know the answer to this question," he said, "but I'm going to ask it anyhow. Why do you plan to kill me?"

"I've got a job," said Colfax.

"Toad and Jasper must be doing pretty well for themselves to be able to hire a mess of would-be killers."

"Who's that?"

"The Jessups," said Luton. "Your bosses."

"Oh," said Colfax, "the Jessups. Yeah. I never heard their given names before. I guess they're doing all right. I don't work cheap."

"Where do they get their money?"

"They got a big ranch outside of Denison. They're new rich, I think. Showed up not too long ago looking like a couple of range bums, but they had a little pocket money.

Somehow or other they got ahold of this big ranch. It used to belong to a fellow named Milam."

"Will Milam?" said Luton.

"Yeah, I think that's his name. Will Milam."

So Toad and Jasper got Will's ranch. God damn those two bastards. Somehow, Luton knew, he had to get past this cold-eyed killer to stop those two.

"What's happened to Milam?" he asked.

"I heard he was over in Henrietta," said Colfax. "I don't know what he's doing there."

"These Jessups," said Luton, "they're not friends of yours?"

"Mr. Luton, I don't have friends. I've never met a man worth calling a friend, and these two are two of the worst I've ever run across."

"But you'd kill a man for them?"

"Not for them. For their money."

Luton's brow furrowed. He had, of course, heard of hired killers, men who killed coldly for money, but he had never talked to one about his work. He was trying hard to dislike this man, but all he could come up with from inside himself was a strong distaste for the man's calling and a powerful, nagging curiosity about the way the man's mind operated on the world.

"Call me 'Sarge,' " said Luton.

Colfax gave Luton a curious look.

"What?" he said.

"If you're going to call me by a name, call me 'Sarge.' Everyone who knows me calls me that."

"Army?" asked Colfax.

"Yeah."

"You'd a been in during the war. Right?"

"That's right."

"Union, right?"

"Right again," said Luton, suddenly feeling a bit antagonistic at this line of questioning. "How'd you guess?"

"It seems like a pretty good reason for an old Texas boy to wind up in Iowa."

"I just couldn't see fighting to tear this country apart," said Luton. "Sam Houston worked hard to get Texas into the United States, and I always stood behind Sam Houston. And I never could go along with the idea that one man could buy and sell another man. So when Texas joined the Confederacy, I went north to Iowa and enlisted up there.

"What do I call you?"

"Cole will do."

"Well, then, Cole," said Luton, "I'm hungry as hell, and I owe you a meal. I understand that this here Katy has got a dining car. Will you join me in tracking it down?"

Colfax stood up.

"After you, Sarge," he said, "or would you feel better if I went first?"

"No, hell, I'll lead the way."

Luton walked to the end of the car and opened the door. For a brief instant he felt foolishly vulnerable with Colfax at his back, but he shrugged off the feeling and stepped out onto the platform. The roar was deafening, and between the two car platforms, Luton could see the ties on the ground rushing past. As he reached for the railing he looked down at the great coupling that held the cars together. He stepped across to the other platform, opened the door to the next car, and stepped inside. He had taken three or four strides down the aisle when a shot rang out behind him. Luton threw himself to the floor and pulled out his Starr revolver. Women screamed around him, and a din of bewildered voices filled the car. Colfax stood just inside the doorway, his Peacemaker in his hand but both hands held up. He was giving Luton a look of caution. On the floor, stretched out in the aisle between them was a man dressed like a cowboy, complete with shotgun chaps. The hair on the right side of his head was matted with blood where Colfax had banged him with the barrel of his Colt. The cowboy's pistol was on the floor just by his outstretched right hand. Luton took it all in in a few seconds and holstered his Starr. He picked up the cowboy's pistol and tucked it in his belt. Colfax holstered his Colt. Just then a conductor came into the car behind Luton.

"What's happening here?" he demanded.

Luton handed the cowboy's pistol, butt first, to the conductor.

"It's all over," he said. "Everything's under control."

A man in a three-piece suit and a derby hat sitting right beside where the unconscious cowboy lay stood up.

"I saw it all," he said. "This gentleman here walked into the car, and just as he was moving down the aisle, this guy on the floor here stood up. He was in the seat right back there. He stood and pulled out a pistol and aimed it at that man's back, but before he could pull the trigger, this other fellow here stepped through the door and knocked him down. He pulled the trigger when he got hit on the head. He was going to murder this man. And this other guy, he saved his life. I was watching the whole thing."

The story was confirmed by several other passengers. The conductor seemed to be satisfied. He knelt over the cowboy, who still had not moved.

"Well," he said, "he's alive. We'll hold him in the baggage car for the authorities at the next stop."

He stood up and faced Colfax.

"I want to thank you, mister. You may have prevented a murder on this train."

"Glad to be of service," said Colfax. "We were just on our way to eat. Mind if we move on?"

"No, no," said the conductor. "Go right ahead."

In the dining car, Luton and Colfax found an unoccupied table and sat down together. A waiter came over with menus.

"Would you gentlemen care for a cocktail?" he said.

"Rye whiskey," said Luton. "Join me?"

"Sure," said Colfax.

The waiter left the menus and went to get the drinks. Luton took a quick look at the menu and tossed it down on the table. The waiter came back with the whiskey.

"I'll have the oyster soup and the quail," said Luton.

"Very good," said the waiter. "You, sir?"

"Same thing," said Colfax.

The waiter went away somewhere to set the meal in motion, and Luton sipped at his whiskey. He put the glass back down on the table and looked at Colfax.

"I don't figure you," he said.

"If I let someone else get you, Sarge, I don't get paid."

"Oh," said Luton, "I see. Just how many of you rascals have the Jessups set on me anyhow?"

"Well, now, that's a funny thing," said Colfax. "It seems they put out the word that they'd pay anyone five hundred dollars to kill you, so there's no way of knowing how many might be after your hide. Then I guess they got nervous. Seemed like a slipshod way of doing business. You don't know who might be after you, but then, neither do they. So they decided to hire a professional."

"You."

"That's right. It will cost them more, but I guarantee my work."

Luton took another sip of whiskey. Colfax was beginning to really exasperate him. He was, in a strange way, likable.

"Cole," he said, "damn it. Do you always get so damned chummy with your intended victims?"

"Not always. Sometimes I know enough about them from the beginning."

"What do you mean? What do you have to know?"

Colfax sipped from his glass, and the waiter brought the soup. The question went unanswered. Luton tasted the oyster soup.

"That's good," he said. *What the hell does he have to know about me that he doesn't know already? How fast I am with a gun? How straight I can shoot? Is he planning some kind of fair fight? A duel? None of this makes any sense.*

Luton finished the rest of his soup and pushed the bowl back away from the edge of the table. Then he finished his whiskey. The waiter came back with the rest of the meal.

"More whiskey, sir?" he said.

"No," said Luton. "I'll have coffee now."

"Me, too," said Colfax.

The waiter hustled off again to fetch the coffee.

"Cole," said Luton, "I want to ask you a question."

"Go ahead."

"How do you sleep at night?"

"Like a baby."

"Doesn't it bother you at all that you make your living by killing innocent people?"

"Everyone I ever killed deserved killing," said Cole. "I made sure. If I didn't know to begin with what they did to deserve it, I found out about them. I haven't yet found an innocent man. Man is evil by nature, Sarge. As the Bard said, 'Use every man after his desert, and who should 'scape whipping?' "

"What?"

"Shakespeare's *Hamlet*. You don't read Shakespeare?"

"No," said Luton impatiently. "I never was much good in school."

"Too bad, but it's too late now anyway. This quail is damn good."

"Cole, I feel sorry for you. If you think that everybody out there is no good, then you've got a damn distorted vision of the world. You've missed out on a lot in your life."

"Oh, I don't know about that," said Colfax, putting down his fork. "Take you, for instance. You must have done something pretty bad to those Jessups for them to go to so much expense to have you killed."

"Well, there you're wrong. I've never done anything to either of the Jessups. That's not why they want me dead."

"Why, then?"

"They want me dead because they know that I want to kill them."

"Then it's self-defense," said Colfax.

Luton thought about Toad and Jessup. He saw his brother's face again, and he recalled digging the shallow grave with his bare hands. He forced the images and the thoughts out of his head.

"You can call it that if it'll ease your conscience," he said.

Chapter Five

Luton suddenly got aggravated with Colfax. He didn't want to talk about what had happened in Texas with anyone, especially not with Colfax. He had never talked about it with anyone in all these years. He had tried over the years to even stop thinking about it—had finally managed to stop the dreams. But the news of the Jessups from Texas had forced the thoughts back into the open. He had even had the dream again. He would not talk about it to Colfax. Not to anyone. Especially not to Colfax. Let Colfax think what he would. He would kill Colfax anyway, would have to, unless Colfax turned out to be quick enough or fast enough or sneaky enough to get him first. Luton realized with a slight shudder that his last thought was entirely possible. Colfax was a cold professional killer, and Luton, as he had been reminded so recently, had grown soft in a comfortable job. He did not like that thought either, but when he tried to shove it out of his mind, the other came back. One unpleasant thought gave way to another, equally unpleasant one.

He called the waiter over to the table and paid for the meals. Then, his own meal only half finished, he shoved his chair back away from the table.

"Colfax," he said, "I'm tired of playing your game. When

you think you're ready, make your move. Meantime leave me alone."

He got up and made his way back to the car where his blanket roll and valise lay on the bench seat, snuggled into the seat as comfortably as he could manage and closed his eyes. Colfax was a strange one. *A hired killer with a conscience,* he thought. *Yes. He's got a conscience. He justifies his profession by telling himself that all mankind is no good, but even then he doesn't believe it, so each time he gets a job, he has to prove his philosophy all over again to himself by finding out some dirt on his intended victim. Well, maybe it will take him long enough to get some dirt on me to let me get my job done. My job.*

The ugly faces of Toad and Jasper Jessup loomed again in his mind, and he thought about when he had first met them. Wichita Falls wasn't much more than a settlement around a trading post that had been established for trade with the Wichita Indians. Bluff Luton and his younger brother, Bud, had ridden in from south Texas on their way toward the Indian Territory. Bluff had heard that there were some large ranchers leasing land from the Cherokees, and he thought that he and his brother might be able to get work as cowboys up there. He wanted to get out of Texas, because there was talk about secession. Texas had just recently gotten itself admitted into the Union. It had been a hard political fight, but they had won it, and only a few years had passed before there was serious talk of pulling out again. Sam Houston had led the movement for Texas statehood, and he led the opposition against secession, but his voice was beginning to sound more and more alone. Bluff Luton agreed with Sam Houston, and he didn't want to deal with what seemed to him almost certain to come about. He took his little brother and headed north.

They had stopped at the small settlement of Wichita Falls to rest and to refresh their trail supplies. They had been there only a short time before they heard the big news. There would be a horse race at the settlement in just one week. Indians would come down across the Red River to take part, and there would be Texans from all over. It was a well-known and well-attended event, and much money would change hands. Bud had grabbed Bluff by the arm and pulled him off to one side when he heard about the race.

"Bluff," he said, "I could enter Sandy Anna in that race. Might even win."

"I don't know, kid," said Bluff. "We got to be moving on. Got a long ways to go yet."

"Hey, Bluff."

"What?"

"Bluff," said Bud, looking into his brother's eyes intently, "Bluff, Sandy can win that race. I know she can. Just give her a chance, will you?"

"Ah, I don't know."

"We got all the money we need?"

"We'll be lucky to have a nickel left when we get to where we're heading," said Bluff.

"Well, all right, then," said Bud, "let me enter the race. It don't cost much, and we stand a good chance to win real big. The purse is five hundred dollars, and there's bets of up to ten thousand."

"How come you know so damn much about it?" said Bluff.

"I just been listening to folks talk around town since we been here."

"Let's go look over the track," said Bluff.

Bud broke into a run.

"Hey, kid," shouted Bluff. "Slow down."

Chapter Six

Colfax finished his meal alone. He didn't rush. Luton had already paid for the meals and the drinks, but Colfax ordered and paid for one more whiskey. While he waited for the waiter to bring it, he rolled himself a cigarette and lit it. He drew deeply on the cigarette and exhaled as the waiter brought his drink. He wished that Bluff Luton hadn't abandoned him. He was beginning to enjoy Luton's company. What the hell, he thought. He'll turn out to be just like all the rest. Scratch a man's surface and you'll find the raw man underneath. Humankind is no better than any other animal. Worse, actually, because humans pretend to be so far above the rest. No one on this earth thinks of anything but self, and those who pretend otherwise, like Bluff Luton, are the worst of the lot, because of the pretense. Greedy animals. All of them. It's greed that keeps this world spinning. Colfax took another drag on his cigarette and thought about Luton. Where was the thin spot on Luton's skin? Where did he have to scratch to expose what was underneath? Well, sooner or later he would find out. He tossed down the whiskey, snuffed out what was left of the cigarette, and got up from the table.

Glancing around the dining car once quickly, he moved to the door and opened it. The roar of the wheels on the tracks

mixed with the creaking and clanking of the coupling between the cars, and as Colfax moved from dining to passenger car, the racket temporarily drove thoughts of Bluff Luton
out of his head. Moving through the passenger car, Cole
again took in the composition of the crowd as he moved
down the aisle. He made his way back to the car where he
and Luton had been sitting earlier and paused just inside the
door. Luton sat in the same seat he had previously occupied.
It was at the opposite end of the car from where Colfax stood
surveying the situation. Luton had made it clear to Colfax
that he wanted no more to do with him until that moment
when Colfax decided to conclude his bloody business, yet
Cole wanted to keep an eye on his prey. There was an empty
bench there beside the door where Colfax lurked, and he
decided that he could watch Luton well enough from that
spot. Just then a small boy, perhaps seven or eight years old,
making train-whistle noises at tremendous volume, ran wildly
down the aisle only to stop abruptly and stare at Colfax's
Colt. Slowly the youngster tilted his head backward until his
large eyes stared into the gray eyes of the killer.

"Oops," he said, and he turned and ran back down the
aisle, reaching the other end of the car just as the train lurched
around a sharp curve in the tracks. The boy fell hard against
the knee of Bluff Luton. Luton reached down to help the boy
to his feet, but the boy took one look at Luton, screamed,
and ran back to the arms of a woman sitting in the middle of
the car. She hugged him to her as he continued to yell. Luton
stood up and followed. He took off his hat as he approached
the woman.

"I'm sorry," she said. "I should have kept him still."

"Oh, that's all right, ma'am," said Luton. "Traveling like
this, I wish I could get up and do that myself. Don't blame
the boy. I hope he's not hurt."

"Oh, no, I'm sure he's not. Just frightened. Thank you
very much."

Luton nodded awkwardly.

"Don't mention it, ma'am," he said, and he turned to go back to his seat.

Colfax sat down on the empty bench at the opposite end of the car. *Damn you, Luton,* he thought. *That was smooth. Be good to kids and ladies. I'll catch you showing your true colors yet, you sly son of a bitch. Did you do that just for my benefit? I bet you did. He probably wanted to slap the shit out of that kid. Way down deep, that's what he really wanted to do. Just slap him across the aisle. Shit.* He pulled the makings out of his pocket and rolled another cigarette. He realized that he had been watching Luton since he had come into the car, and Luton had not looked around. He couldn't have known that Colfax had come into the car. Of course, Luton couldn't have put on a show with the boy and the woman for the benefit of Colfax, not knowing that Colfax was there. *Just relax,* he said to himself. *There's no damn hurry. He'll show himself. Relax and wait it out.* He took a small tin box out of his pocket and slid back the lid. He took a match out of the box, closed the lid, replaced the box in his pocket, and struck the match on the back of the bench in front of him. Lighting the cigarette, he drew deeply, filling his lungs with smoke.

Just before Bluff Luton had returned to his seat, as he was nodding to the woman with the crying boy, he had seen Colfax at the rear of the car. He did his best not to let the gunman know that he had seen him, or at least, to make him think that if he had seen him, he had not given him serious notice. He was glad for the episode of the stumbling kid, though, for it had brought his mind back to the present. He had been dwelling on the past for too long, he thought. *Much too long. That damned Colfax anyhow. I told him to keep away, so he sits there in the back of the car and stares at me.* Luton imagined that he could feel the stare of the gray eyes on the back of his head. He fought off an urge to turn around and look at Colfax. *Damn him.* In an effort to drive the annoyance of Colfax out of his thoughts, Luton tried to picture the

woman he had just spoken to. He hadn't stared at her. He
had, in fact, avoided looking directly at her, but he had gotten
a strong impression. She was a good-looking woman, he
thought. A woman, not a girl. She must be around thirty.
The kid, he was almost sure, was her son. Then she had a
husband somewhere, but the husband didn't seem to be along
on this trip. She was traveling alone with her young son.
Heading for Texas. Maybe the husband had gone to Texas
ahead of his family to get established, and now he had sent
for them to join him. What color was her hair? Luton couldn't
remember. Her eyes? No. He hadn't really looked. But she
looked strong. He had that impression. She wasn't skinny.
She had been wearing—he couldn't remember—a dress. She
had been wearing a dress and she had a kid—a snotnosed,
wild, running and screaming little kid who had run into his
knee and given him a bruise. The back door of the car opened
and Luton turned to see the conductor stroll in.

"Nevada, Missouri, just ahead," droned the conductor.
"We'll stop for twenty minutes. You can eat in the depot if
you're a mind to."

The depot in Nevada was just like the other one Luton had
experienced. This time he did for himself what Colfax had
done for him before. He made sure that his coffee cup was
clean and his food was fresh. People were elbowing and shoving each other in an attempt to get to the counter. Just as Luton
was raising his cup to take a sip of coffee, someone slammed
into him from behind. Luton put the cup down and turned on
his stool. The culprit was a pompous-looking middle-aged
man in a three-piece suit and derby. Luton reached out and
took the handkerchief out of the man's breast pocket.

"Hey," said the man.

"You spilled it," said Luton, using the handkerchief to
mop up the coffee on the counter in front of him.

"Now just a minute."

"Just a minute to you," said Luton. "I expect you to pay
for this coffee."

"You can go straight to hell."

Luton pulled the Starr out of his holster and jammed it into the man's paunch.

"Just put your money on the counter," he said.

The man did as he was told and backed away into the crowd. As Luton shoved the Starr back into the holster, he saw the woman from the train back in the crowd. She was looking longingly toward the counter but with a kind of hopeless exasperation. The boy was clinging to her skirts. Luton stood up and shoved the most immediate of the crowd aside.

"Ma'am," he said, "there's a place right up here."

She tried to take a step forward, but the crowd was too thick in front of her. Luton felt himself reaching the end of his patience. The reminders of the past, the task awaiting him at the end of his journey, the long train ride, the annoyance of hired killers along the way, including Colfax—no, especially Colfax—and the general rudeness of the travelers combined to make him want to begin flailing out with his fists. He stepped forward, shoving a few more people out of the way.

"Here," he said, "let the lady through. Get out of the way."

The lady and her small companion stepped through the crowd and up toward the counter, but as Luton turned, a young man quickly slid onto the stool he had vacated.

"I got up from there to make room for this lady," said Luton.

"You got up," said the other.

"It's all right," said the lady.

"I'm hungry," whined the boy.

"No, ma'am, excuse me," said Luton, "but it's not all right."

He turned back to the young man on the stool.

"Get up," he said.

The young man turned to face Luton, probably intending to make some bold reply, but he hesitated when he looked into Luton's face. His mouth hung open for an instant. Then he stood up.

"Yeah. Sure," he said, and he, too, vanished into the crowd.

"You can sit right here, ma'am," said Luton.

"My son is very hungry," said the lady. "Climb up there, Matt."

The boy scrambled up onto the stool. A man sitting on the next stool to the boy's right, who had watched the whole incident with interest, backed off his stool. He looked, not at the lady, but at Luton.

"The lady can have this place," he said.

"Thank you," said Luton. "Ma'am."

The lady sat down next to young Matt, and Luton waved a waiter over and placed an order for them. The plates and cups were hardly on the counter before the conductor stepped in at a side door, pulled a big watch out of his pocket, gave it a cursory glance, and then yelled, "All aboard."

The crowd rushed for the doors. People at the counter took last, desperate slurps and gulps of their cups of coffee and tea. Young Matt turned to the lady with an anxious look on his face.

"Mom?" he said.

Luton looked at the big clock on the wall.

"Excuse me, ma'am," he said. "You two finish your meal. It's all right."

The crowd had almost dissipated, and Luton stalked across the depot floor to where the conductor had just turned and started for the train. Luton grabbed him by a shoulder and spun him around.

"What the hell?" said the conductor.

"Mister," said Luton, "we were promised twenty minutes here. It has not yet been twenty minutes. I suspect that these food merchants, who I know try to sell the same food over again, have paid you to run everyone out of here early. Now, there's a young lady over there at the counter with her young son. They're traveling alone. I would not like to see them have to board the train hungry. And I promise you, if you make them miss the train, you'll regret it."

The conductor gave Luton a quick study.

"They'll be all right," he said. "There's time."

"Thank you," said Luton.

The conductor went on outside, and Luton went back to the counter. He walked up to a stool beside the one where the lady sat.

"May I?" he said.

"Oh, certainly," said the lady. "Please do."

Luton sat down.

"My name is Bluff Luton, ma'am," he said, "but most folks call me 'Sarge.' "

"I'm Emily Fisher, and this is Matt."

Matt was busy with a large cinnamon roll, but he did manage to roll his eyes toward Luton.

"Howdy, Matt," said Luton.

Matt said something through his roll.

"Thank you for helping us out," said Emily. "I think we'd never have gotten anything to eat otherwise."

"Oh, that's all right, ma'am," said Luton. "Folks ought to have better manners. It makes me wonder how they were brought up."

Luton motioned toward a waiter.

"Get me another cup of coffee," he said.

The waiter brought one and set it down in front of Luton, but before he could speak, Luton did.

"No charge," he said. "I didn't finish my meal awhile ago, and I saw you resell it. I will pay for these two, though."

"Oh, no," said Emily, "please. You've done quite enough."

Luton paid the waiter.

"It's all right," he said. "After all the commotion I caused in here, I kind of feel responsible."

It was funny, he thought. He did kind of feel responsible, and he wondered why. This woman and her son were of no significance to him. He did hate to see women treated rudely, but wasn't it enough that he had seen to it that they had a place to eat and time enough to finish their meal? Did he have to pay for their food? The woman was obviously married and was probably going to Texas to join her husband. Well, it didn't matter. Luton wasn't after anything from the lady. He was just helping out a little. Emily and Matt finished their meal, and Luton his coffee. He escorted them out to the train, purposefully maintaining a leisurely pace. As he stood at the bottom of the steps waiting for Emily and Matt to climb aboard, he smiled and nodded at the conductor, who was standing impatiently by. Then Luton mounted the steps.

Inside the car, Emily and Matt had just taken their seats. There was a space beside Emily. Luton hesitated and looked around the car. Colfax was conspicuous by his absence.

"Please sit down, Mr. Luton," said Emily.

"Thank you, ma'am, but I wish you wouldn't call me 'mister.' Just call me 'Sarge' or 'Bluff' if you prefer."

"All right, Sarge, on one condition. I'm Emily."

"Yes, ma'am," said Luton. "Uh, excuse me. Emily."

"She's my mom," said Matt.

"You're a lucky boy to have such a fine mama."

Emily flushed slightly at the compliment.

"Are you traveling on business, Sarge?" she asked.

"Yes, you might say that."

"What kind of business are you in?"

"Well, actually, I'm a town marshal," said Luton. "At Riddle, a little town up in Iowa. The reason I'm traveling, I guess you could call it personal business."

"Oh, I didn't mean to pry."

"No, that's all right. I just took some time off from my job for the first time in years."

"Being a town marshal must be very dangerous work."

"Not really. Riddle is a quiet little town."

"Are you really a marshal?" said Matt.

"Yes, I'm afraid so, son," said Luton.

"Do you kill bad men?"

"Matt," said Emily.

"I try not to," said Luton. He thought of Toad and Jasper and how he wanted to kill them, how he intended to kill them, and he felt a pang of guilt—not because of the desire, but because of the lie.

"Why not, if they're bad?"

"I try to put them in jail or just make them get out of town."

"Then why do you have that gun?"

"Well," said Luton, "sometimes they just won't listen, so I have to be ready, just in case."

"You ask too many questions, Matt," said Emily. "Now be still."

"It's all right," said Luton. "A boy's just naturally curious. Are you bound for Texas?"

"Yes, we're going to Henrietta."

"Well, I reckon I'll be traveling with you most of the way. I'm going to Wichita Falls."

"Do the tracks go there?"

"No. At least, the last I knew they didn't. I think I'll have to catch a ride over from Henrietta. But that's pretty close."

"Yes," said Emily. "It's only a little ways from there."

"Do you know Texas?"

"Yes."

"Your home?"

"My father lives in Henrietta."

"Oh," said Luton, "you're taking the boy for a visit to his grandpa?"

"No, we're going to stay."

"I'm sorry," said Luton. "I didn't mean to pry."

Emily laughed, and Luton liked the sound of her laughter. It relaxed him.

"It seems like I just said that," she said. "It's all right. I'm a divorced woman, Sarge. My husband was a cruel man. He mistreated me and my son. We lived in Boston, and I divorced him, and I'm taking my son with me back to Texas."

"I'm sorry to hear that. I can't understand a man like that."

"Well, it's all over now."

"Yes, ma'am."

"Emily," she corrected.

"Emily."

Luton wondered what kind of a man could be cruel to such a woman. He couldn't stomach the idea of a man's mistreating any woman. Such a man, in the mind of Luton, deserved no consideration whatsoever. He should be shot down like a dog. But for a man to be so fortunate as to have a woman like this one for his wife, and then to mistreat her when what he should be doing was caring for her, such a man was unthinkable. Luton found himself wishing that he could confront this man, wanting to smash in his face. He tried to imagine what that face would look like. He would probably be a handsome man, one no one would suspect of secret cruelty. Slick. Slimy. Now there was one more ugly thought to torment the mind of Luton on this seemingly interminable ride. *Goddamn it*, he thought, *I wish to God this was all over with. Riddle will sure seem nice to get back to.*

"Can I see your gun?" said Matt.

"No, son," said Luton, coming out of his reverie, "I don't think that would be a good idea."

"Why not?"

The near door opened, and Colfax stepped into the car, facing Luton and his new traveling companions. He had heard Matt's questions, and he stepped over to the boy. Pulling his Colt out, he handed it to Matt.

"Here," he said. "Take a look at this one."

"Matt, don't," said Emily.

Matt had the big gun in his small hands.

"Hell, it's all right," said Colfax. "He can't pull that hammer back."

Luton jerked the Starr revolver out of his holster and held it leveled at Colfax's belly.

"Take your revolver and get out of here, Cole," he said.

Colfax laughed, then reached for the Colt. Matt hardly gripped it. His big eyes were on the Starr in Luton's hand. Cole holstered his Colt, tipped his hat to Emily, and walked to the other end of the car, where he found himself a seat. Luton put away his Starr and heaved a long sigh.

"I'm sorry about that, Emily," he said.

"A friend of yours?"

"Not really. I just met him on the train."

Matt sat quietly staring at Luton, still stunned by what he had just seen, and Luton settled back into the seat to try to relax. He had a feeling inside him that said that he had never really been out of Oliver Colfax's sight. Not for a minute.

Chapter Seven

The back of Luton's neck burned from the feeling that Colfax was staring at him from the other end of the car. He'd have to try to put that son of a bitch out of his mind. He believed Colfax when the killer said he would let Luton know when he was ready to finish his job. He couldn't come up with a good reason for believing him, but he did. So why worry about him in the meantime? Colfax wouldn't shoot him in the back without any warning. He knew that. Still, it bothered him to have the man around, constantly watching him, studying, calculating. What was he thinking? And why was it so important to him to discover some flaw in Luton's character before trying to kill him? Damn him, Luton thought. To hell with him.

The roar from the wheels on the tracks became louder as someone opened the door at the far end of the car. Luton glanced over his shoulder. He didn't recognize the man who came into the car and shut the door behind himself. Before he turned his head back around, Luton noticed that Colfax sat with his hat down over his eyes. He appeared to be napping. At least he wasn't just staring at Luton's back. Luton relaxed a little. The stranger who had come into the car didn't appear to be anyone to worry about. Luton guessed from his clothes that he was an Easterner. He was a young man. Looks like a bank teller, Luton thought. Just about then the young man stepped past Luton, stopped, and turned around. Luton tensed again, waiting for the man's next move, but the man looked right past Luton.

"Well, hello there, Miz Fisher," he said, touching the brim of his natty little dark brown derby.

Luton saw Emily stiffen. Her cheeks colored slightly.

"Ryan," she said. "What are you doing here?"

The man called Ryan ignored her question.

"Hi there, Matthew," he said. "How are you today?"

"I'm fine," said the boy.

Young Matt did not look as if he had meant what he said. There was fear in his large eyes.

"Ryan," Emily repeated, "why are you here?"

"Why, George sent me, of course," said the Easterner. "I work for George."

"But why?"

Ryan looked around. The only seat not taken was the one on which Luton's saddle roll and valise were stashed. He pushed them off onto the floor and sat down, putting a foot on top of the roll.

"That's my gear, mister," said Luton. "Take your foot off it."

George lifted his foot as Luton picked up the roll and valise and stood to secure them on the overhead shelf. Luton sat back down.

"Miz Fisher," said Ryan, "George sent me to bring you back home. You and little Matthew."

"We're not going," said Emily.

"George won't take that for an answer. I'm afraid that I have to take you back with me."

"You get out of here and leave us alone."

"Sorry. I can't do that."

Luton decided that he had heard enough.

"Mister," he said, "you get up and go on back to wherever you came from. At the next stop you get off of this train."

Ryan slowly turned his face toward Luton. He let out a long, exasperated sigh.

"Listen, hayseed," he said, "this is none of your business. I work for the woman's husband. Why don't you just go find yourself another seat and forget all about her."

"She said she's not going with you," said Luton. "Move on."

Ryan leaned back and looked at Luton for a moment. Then he glanced at Emily with an ugly sneer forming on his young face. He laughed.

"Oh, I get it," he said. "You're the lady's protector. George is going to find this very interesting. How's she paying you? With a roll in the hay?"

"Now that's enough," said Luton.

"I'm going to tell you one more time, hick," said Ryan, shaking a finger in Luton's face, "stay out of things that are none of your business. Mr. Fisher is a powerful man. I'm giving you some good advice."

Luton reached out and grabbed the finger, twisting it backward. Ryan screamed with pain and leaned over in a back bend across the bench seat behind him until his head touched the wall. Luton kept the pressure on the finger. His face came close to Ryan's.

"Mister," he said, "I don't know your Mr. Fisher. I don't care to know him, and I don't care who or what he is. I will tell you one time that there is nothing between me and this lady, but I will also tell you that where I come from a man doesn't bully a lady. Now move over."

By twisting Ryan's finger, Luton made Ryan move out into the aisle, then backed him up against the door. With his left hand he reached around behind his victim and opened the door, then moved out with him onto the platform between the two cars. He shut the door behind them. Ryan looked with fear in his eyes down at the ties speeding along beneath them. He tried to say something to Luton, but the pain in his finger and the roar of the wheels on the tracks prevented it. Luton gave the finger a final wrenching and shoved Ryan across the platform into the opposite door.

"Can you hear me?" he shouted.

"Yes."

"The next time you bother that lady, I'll throw you off of this train. I suggest you find another car and get off at the next stop."

Ryan's face was white with fear, and Luton was sure that he had seen the last of the man, but just as he started to turn to go back inside the car, the Easterner reached inside his coat and produced a pocket derringer. Luton dropped quickly to a squatting position just in time to duck the shot. With all the strength of his legs, he lunged upward and across the platform, flinging his weight into Ryan. Ryan's pocket pistol clattered onto the platform. Luton pressed Ryan against the door and slapped him across the face. Then he turned the man and forced him into the guardrail at the side of the platform. Luckily for Ryan the train was making a curve and climbing a grade at the same time. It was not much of a grade, but it was enough to have slowed the progress a bit. The ground looked hard and rocky, and it sloped down away from the tracks. Luton clutched Ryan's collar at the back of the neck with his left hand while his right grabbed a handful of material at the seat of the pants. He heaved with all his might, and Ryan screamed as his body arced out into space, arms flailing at the wind. Luton watched him hit and bounce and begin rolling down the hill. Then he turned and went back inside the car.

"He won't be bothering you anymore," he said to Emily Fisher as he sat down beside her.

"What did you do to Ryan?" said Matt, his eyes wide with expectation.

"I didn't hurt him much," said Luton. "I just asked him to get off the train."

"I don't know how to thank you," said Emily.

"Don't try. I didn't do much. A man out here just naturally

takes up for a lady. Besides, I just didn't like that weasel's looks.''

Luton leaned back in his seat and wondered where they were. He thought that they should be crossing into Kansas sometime soon. After that they would go into Indian Territory, crossing the Cherokee, Creek, and Choctaw nations and a small patch of the Chickasaw Nation before getting into Texas. It was a long trip, and he would be glad when it was over. Before then, however, there would be Colfax to deal with. And there would be the Jessups—Toad and Jasper. They were the whole reason for the trip in the first place. *Damn*, he thought, *that damn Colfax and that weasel Ryan have almost made me forget why I'm doing this.* Then he remembered that he had wanted ways of keeping his mind off the reason—to keep it off the past and to keep out the unpleasant memories. In Texas, if he made it to Texas, if he could get past Colfax and his Colt, he would see Toad and Jasper, and he would kill them, or they would kill him. Then it would all be over. Over. After all these years. Finally over. And he would see Will Milam again, he thought. That would be nice, to see Will again. And then another thought occurred to him, and he wondered why he had not considered it before. When all this was over, he would not see Emily again. Suddenly he was no longer so sure that he was anxious for this trip to end.

Bud Luton sat a horse well. Bluff had to admit that, and when the boy got onto the back of Sandy, well, there just wasn't much that could keep up with them. That Sandy was some horse. A dun mare that was long and lean, Sandy was young Bud's pride. He had thought that her dun color looked like the sand along the Gulf and so he had called her Sandy. Then he had thought that it would be clever to turn the horse's name into a pun on the name of Texas's most hated and feared recent enemy. Therefore, her full name became Sandy Anna. Yes, Bud and Sandy would be hard to beat. Even so, Bluff didn't like hanging around the little settlement of

Wichita Falls for the day of the race. He wanted to get on out of Texas and find jobs for himself and Bud on some cozy cattle outfit somewhere up in the Indian Territory. Big ranchers had leased land from the Cherokees, he had heard, and things were booming up there. Still, Bud wanted to run Sandy Anna in this race in the worst way, and Sandy was a good horse. With Bud on her back, she just might win. And they were just about busted. It might be a more pleasant trip with a little money in their pockets. So they hung around Wichita Falls, Bud working with Sandy, studying the track, watching the other horses and riders as they showed up and announced, and making a few new acquaintances along the way. Will Milam was one. Will was about the same age as Bluff, and the two young men took a liking to each other right away.

"Why don't you stay here and throw in with me?" Will had said. "You'll never get rich working for someone else. We'll start our own ranch."

But Bluff had his mind set on the Indian Territory and on getting out of Texas, and, although he never voiced it to Will or to Bud or to anyone else, for that matter, the idea of going into business for himself scared him. It was too big, and Bluff Luton just didn't have any big ideas. No, he told Will. He and Bud would just move on when the big race was over. Win or lose, they would continue their trip to the Indian Territory and look for ranch work up there.

"Well," Will had said, "if you ever change your mind, come on back down here and look me up. I'll have the biggest spread in these parts."

"Yeah?" said Bluff. "Well, okay, but if you go busted, you come on up to the Nations and look up me and Bud."

Will had made good on his plans. He had developed one of the biggest and best cattle ranches in north Texas. Over the years word had gotten to Bluff Luton and he knew about it. He had often wondered whether or not he had been stupid when he had turned down Milam's offer of partnership. But then Luton's admonition to Milam had, according to Luton's latest information, turned out to be prophetic after all. It had taken a good many years, but Milam had lost his ranch after all. And lost it to the Jessups. Goddamn those Jessups. The faces of Toad and Jasper loomed up in Luton's mind as he dozed in the Katy car racing toward Texas.

At the opposite end of the car, Oliver Colfax slumped against the back of the bench seat, his Montana peak hat pulled down over his eyes. He was not asleep. He was resting. But even in his rest, Colfax thought. Here on the Katy he thought of Bluff Luton. He had known about Bluff Luton, the man they called "Sarge," for some years now. He had the reputation of a tough but fair lawman—a man to steer clear of or to get along with. Colfax respected the man's reputation, but he also knew that for several years Luton had presided over a quiet and law-abiding town. Probably he had gotten soft. The skills of violence, Colfax knew, required constant honing. He was not afraid of Luton or his reputation, yet Luton bothered him. Colfax was able to follow his chosen profession because of a solid philosophical belief in the innate depravity of man. He had never known a good man. He was firmly convinced that any human being, if watched closely enough for a sufficiently long period of time, would reveal himself to be as degenerate as all the rest. He was watching Luton. Luton was smooth, Colfax thought. He was slow to anger. He went out of his way to help women and children. *Yeah*, he said to himself, *he's a smooth one, but I'll catch him at something*.

> *When he is drunk asleep, or in his rage . . .*
> *At gaming, swearing, or about some act*
> *That has no relish of salvation in't;*
> *Then trip him, that his heels may kick at heaven,*
> *And that his soul may be as damn'd and black*
> *As hell, where to it goes.*

There was the matter of Luton's present pilgrimage, a trip with no other purpose than to kill two men, but Luton hadn't

told Colfax enough about his reasons for wanting to do this
slaughter. He knew those two men, the Jessups, and he could
think of few men he had ever met who needed killing more
than they. Possibly they had done something in the past to
Luton, or more likely in his case, to someone Luton cared
about, which would justify this seeming evil. Colfax needed
to know why Luton wanted to kill the Jessups. If Luton's
reason was good, he would have to search farther for evidence of the man's clay feet, but clay they would be. Colfax
was sure of that.

Chapter Eight

Matthew Fisher was restless. He thought that the train ride would never end, and he wanted to get up and run and play. He wriggled around in his seat. He scratched his leg. He had quietly sung the alphabet song to himself three times. He thought about walking to the other end of the car, but he had seen the man with the big gun sitting back there—the one that Mr. Luton had chased away—and he was afraid to get close to him. His mother and Mr. Luton were both asleep, and he didn't want to wake either one of them. He looked out the window and watched trees and hills rush past him on their way to where he had been already. He breathed on the window and drew squiggly lines in the dampness that his breath had left there. Finally, no longer able to contain himself, he got up quietly, careful not to disturb the two sleepers, and walked into the aisle. He made his way about halfway down the aisle toward the far end of the car. The man with the big gun sat slumped in his seat with his hat brim down over his eyes. Matt turned and walked back to where his mother and Mr. Luton slept. He looked at them, wishing that one of them would wake up. Then he walked to the door.

Suddenly he felt very bold, and he opened the door and stepped out onto the platform, pulling the door shut behind

himself. The train seemed to lurch much more out on the
platform than it did inside the car, and the noise from the
roar of the engine and from the wheels on the tracks was
almost deafening. Just then the train whistled, and Matt
pressed his back up against the door. His eyes were wide and
he could feel his heart pounding in his little chest. He looked
down between the platforms of the two cars and watched with
horrified fascination the rushing of the ground and the railroad ties beneath him, and he wondered with excited terror
if Mr. Luton had thrown Ryan down there to be ground up
by the big wheels. Then he saw the gun there on the platform.
It was not a big gun like that strange man had—not even as
big as Mr. Luton's gun—although Mr. Luton had not let him
hold his gun or even look at it. But it was a gun. It was a real
gun. He was sure of that. He wanted the gun, but he was
afraid to move. The roar was so loud and the lurching was
so violent. But he wanted the gun. It just lay there waiting
for him to pick it up, shining and slick. It looked cold and
hard, and it was so small that it wouldn't be heavy like that
other one. He would be able to handle this one.

Slowly Matthew slid his back down the door until he was
on his knees. Then he reached forward to get his hands on
the jerking platform. That put his face closer to the racing
ground down there, and it scared him, but he pulled his eyes
away from the frightening chasm between the platforms and
fastened them once again on the gun. He crawled forward,
inching his way along the hard steel, and pain shot through
his bony knees, but finally his right hand reached out and
grasped the gun. He made his way back to the door and sat
down, his back securely pressed once again to the door. He
held the gun in his hands, and he found that it was cold and
hard, and he thought that it was beautiful. He put his small
thumb on the hammer and pulled, but he wasn't strong
enough to cock the thing. He rubbed it all over, savoring the
different feel of the steel barrel and the polished wood grip,
then he dropped it in his jacket pocket and sheepishly made
his way back inside the car.

* * *

It was about twenty miles ahead of the train on a rocky and wooded hillside overlooking the tracks where four horseback riders bunched up. Below the riders a water tank stood beside the tracks just where they leveled off following a long, gradual grade uphill. The leader of this motley band, a man who called himself Randall Lee Bow, his family a generation or two back having totally lost touch with its French roots, looked down on the tracks. Randall Lee, as he was sometimes called, was flanked by Joe Don Tucker and the brothers, Harlan and Odie Bass. They waited for the train.

"You sure that train's going to stop here, Randall Lee?" asked Tucker.

"You see that hill yonder it's got to climb?" asked Randall Lee.

"Yeah."

"You see that there windmill and that water tank?"

"Yeah, I see them."

"Well," said Randall Lee, "if you knowed anything about trains, you'd know that it's got to stop here."

"A train's kind of like a horse, Joe Don," said Harlan Bass. "It's got to take on water after a long climb. Ain't that right, Randall Lee?"

"A train ain't nothing like a horse, you dummy," said Randall Lee.

Odie Bass laughed, a high-pitched giggle, and slapped his brother across the shoulder.

"Of course it ain't," he said. "Any damn fool knows that. A horse ain't got wheels."

"Hell," said Harlan, his face flushed with embarrassment, "I know a horse ain't got wheels. That ain't what I meant. What I meant was that if you work a horse hard you got to give him a drink of water. Well, don't you?"

"Yeah, I reckon," said Joe Don.

"And if you drive a train up a long hill, you got to give it water, too. Don't you? That's what Randall Lee said. Ain't it? Well?"

"That's what he said," said Joe Don.

"Well, hell, that's all I meant. What the hell's wrong with that?"

Odie shrieked again like a hyena.

"Horse like a train," he said. "Horse like a train. Shit. I wonder how many legs that train's got that we're awaiting for. How many, you think, Randall Lee?"

"Shut up. All of you," said Randall Lee. "That train's going to be along here pretty soon now. We got to get set. Luton ain't no man to fool around with. This job calls for careful planning."

"How we going to kill him, Randall Lee?" said Joe Don.

"Study the lay of the land," said Randall Lee. "That train's going to stop so that its engine is right along side of that tower. They got to pull that snout down to water it. The passenger cars'll be strung out along the track on back of it there. Some of the passengers'll get off to walk around and stretch their legs when the train stops. Some won't. We got to watch and see if Luton gets off."

"What if he don't?"

"Shut up. I'll get to that. If we see him get off, we just blast away at him. If he don't get off, we'll have to make him get off. Joe Don, I want you and Odie to get on that windmill over there. Odie can get down behind the beams and you can climb up on top. When them train men starts to water the engine, you cover them. All you do is just keep them still until I say let them go."

"Why can't me and Harlan do that?" said Odie.

"Because you and Harlan can't keep still whenever you're together. Just do as I say."

"Okay. Hell."

"Harlan, you get in them bushes down there. You'll have a good shot at the passengers."

"Them's sticker bushes, Randall Lee," Harlan protested.

"They won't kill you, but Luton might. Just do as I say."

"Sticker bushes," mumbled Harlan.

"I'm going to be behind that big rock right over yonder,

and I don't want none of you to do nothing but just to keep everybody covered. Leave it all to me. Don't shoot unless I yell at you to. You got that? I'm just going to get that Luton off the train and tell them train men to get on out of here. Then we'll kill him and take him on down to the Jessups to get our money."

"Randall Lee," said Odie, "I hear the train."

"Shut up."

Randall Lee cocked his head and listened. He could hear the sound of the locomotive puffing its way up the long grade.

"Yeah," he said, "it's acoming. Now take your positions and keep quiet and keep out of sight until I show myself. Then you show yourselfs and show that we've got everybody covered. Now git."

"Randall Lee?" said Harlan.

"What?"

"What about the horses?"

Randall Lee showed a moment's hesitation before he regained his composure.

"Why, take them down there in the brush and hide them, of course. Do I have to tell you every little move to make? Get going."

Harlan led the four horses into the thick brush and tied them. Then he fought his way on into the bushes where he had been told to wait. His clothes caught on the stickers.

"Shit," he said, as he felt a tug on his right sleeve. He pulled the sleeve to free it from a slender branch, and as it pulled loose the branch swung upward and scratched his face. Harlan screamed.

"Keep quiet down there," yelled Randall Lee.

"I'm getting all scratched up in here," said Harlan.

"Just shut up."

Odie crouched down behind the framework of the windmill and watched Joe Don climb up to peer around the blades as they revolved slowly in the easy breeze. Joe Don had a good view of the water tower just below them.

"Damn," said Joe Don. "It's cold up here."

Randall Lee stood up from behind his rock and shouted. "Goddamn it. Everybody shut up and keep quiet."

The train had slowed down considerably as it labored up the long grade. Emily straightened herself up, stretching slightly, coming out of a nap. Matthew had not moved since coming back inside with the derringer hidden in his pocket. He looked up at his mother.

"Why are we going slow?" he asked.

"Well," said Emily, "I suppose it's because we're climbing a hill. The train can't climb a hill as fast as it can move along on flat ground."

"Oh."

Matthew opened the window to stick his head out and look, and a blast of cold air came into the car.

"Matt," said Emily, "don't do that. Close the window. It's too cold out."

"I just want to look."

"Well, look through the window. Keep it shut."

Matthew shut the window and sat back in the seat. He thought about the gun in his pocket and decided that he'd better be good. Then Bluff Luton stirred and yawned, and Matt was certain that his best behavior was called for.

"Did you have a good nap, Sarge?" said Emily.

Luton stretched, and as he did, he sneaked a look over his shoulder. Colfax was gone. He was nowhere to be seen. *Damn,* thought Luton. *I don't know whether it's more aggravating to have him back there watching me or to not know where he's at.*

"Yeah," he said. "Thank you."

The conductor walked into the car, shouting for attention.

"Water stop ahead, folks. It'll take a few minutes to fill 'er up. You're welcome to get out and walk around if you've a mind to."

Luton looked at Emily.

"Do you think that you'd like to get out and walk around a bit?" he said.

"What's there?" she asked.

"Just a water tank, I reckon. It's just a water stop. For the train."

"Oh, thank you," said Emily, "but I really don't think so. It's beginning to get chilly out there."

"I want to get out," said Matt.

"Oh, Matt, I don't know."

"I'll be happy to take the boy out," said Luton. "It might do us both some good."

Randall Lee Bow's heart was pounding as the train pulled up to the water tank and finally came to a stop. He hoped that his boys would do as they had been told. He watched as a train man climbed up on top to pull down the water snout from the tank. Harlan was hidden in his sticker bush. Randall Lee looked toward the windmill. He could see Odie and Joe Don, but that was probably because he knew where to look. He knew they were there. No one else had noticed them yet. He watched as a small boy came running off one of the passenger cars, followed by a big man. From the other end of the same car, two men stepped out on the ground. A train man stepped out of another car, followed by a few more passengers. Randall Lee began to panic. Things were getting out of control. Quickly he stepped out from behind his rock, his six-gun leveled at the largest group of passengers.

"Everyone hold still," he shouted. "Boys, show yourselfs."

Harlan stood up in the midst of his sticker bush, gun in hand, sleeve caught on some stickers. Odie peered from around the framework of the windmill, and Joe Don stood up on top.

"We got you covered," Randall Lee hollered. "All we want is Bluff Luton. We get him, won't nobody else get hurt."

Matt had run out ahead of Luton, and he was standing between Luton and Randall Lee. Luton walked toward Matt.

"Hold it, mister," shouted Randall Lee.

"I'm Luton. Let these people get back inside."

"All right," said Randall Lee, "but you stay."

"I'll stay, but first I want to put this boy back on the train."

"Shuck your hardware," said Randall Lee.

Luton opened his coat wide, showing the Starr revolver. Then with his left hand he reached for it slowly, pulled it out, and dropped it to the ground.

"I'm putting this boy on the train," he said.

"Go on," said Randall Lee, "but you put one foot up on a step and I'll shoot a hole in your back."

Luton walked to Matt and picked him up. He turned his back on Randall Lee and walked toward the train.

"Don't be afraid, Matt," he said. "You'll be all right. When I put you on the steps, you go on inside to your mother and stay there."

"You threw your gun down," said Matt.

"Yeah, I had to. I don't want you to get hurt."

"All right," shouted Randall Lee, "everyone but Luton get back inside. Now."

The passengers and the conductor who had disembarked turned and made their way back into the cars. The man on top whose job it was to get the water had dropped down out of sight. Luton placed Matt on the platform.

"Now go on in," he said.

"Sarge?" said Matt.

"It's okay, boy, go on inside."

"Sarge, I've got a gun."

"What?"

"In my coat pocket. It's just a little one."

Luton felt Matt's pockets and found the derringer. It must be Ryan's, he thought. He hoped there was a bullet in it. Ryan had fired only once, and Luton knew that the little gun held two shots. He reached into Matt's pocket and palmed the small weapon, then patted Matt with his left hand.

"Go on," he said.

Matt turned and ran to the door as Luton turned back around to face his captors.

"Come on, Luton," said Randall Lee. "Come on."

Luton walked toward Randall Lee. He hadn't quite reached the spot where he had dropped his Starr when Randall Lee stopped him.

"That's far enough. Put your hands up over your head."

Luton reached forward with both hands, slowly raising them, but when they were parallel to the ground and outstretched before him, his right hand twisted and the derringer flashed. Randall Lee screamed and grabbed for his chest. Luton made a dive for the Starr. Harlan Bass screamed in fear, turned, and ripped his way through the sticker bush, tearing clothing and flesh in his flight. He ran for the horses. Luton rolled, picking up his Starr and turning to level it at Randall Lee. He saw that Randall Lee had dropped his gun and was sinking to his knees. He did not fire a second shot. He could tell there was no need. From atop the windmill, Joe Don began firing wildly in Luton's direction. The back door of the dining car opened, and Colfax stepped out, took careful aim with his Colt, and blew Joe Don off the tower. Joe Don's left foot caught in the framework as he fell backward, and he was left hanging grotesquely above Odie Bass. Odie gasped, backed around behind the windmill, then ran for the bushes.

Luton stepped on over to where Randall Lee had fallen. One look told him that his shot had done the job. Randall Lee Bow was dead. Colfax strolled over to Luton.

"I knocked one off that windmill over there," he said. "Two others ran for the hills."

"Yeah," said Luton, "I saw it."

"You want to go after those two?"

"Naw, they ain't worth the time. To hell with them."

Luton looked at Colfax. He wondered if he should thank the man for helping him out, even though he knew that Colfax had done so only to save him for himself—when he felt the time was right. Luton decided against it. To hell with him, too, he said to himself.

"That was a smooth move you made, Sarge," said Colfax. "Say, where'd you get that peashooter, anyway?"

Luton tossed the derringer in the air and caught it. He dropped it into his pocket and thought about Matt.

"Off that dude I tossed overboard," he said.

Chapter Nine

Odie Bass ran for his life. He stumbled on the rocks getting up the side of the hill, and he skinned his knees on the rough, sharp edges of stone. Looking back over his shoulder at one point, he ran into a tree, bruising the side of his face. He ran over the top of the hill and he kept running until he thought that his lungs would burst. Then he fell. He waited, expecting someone to come up on him at any moment and kill him. He wondered whether they would just shoot him in the back as he lay there or drag him to his feet and hang him from the nearest suitable tree branch. He had seen Randall Lee fall, and then Joe Don had been left hanging upside down just above his own head. He couldn't run for the horses without crossing in front of the man who had killed Joe Don and then running past Luton. God, he wanted his horse. Or any horse.

As his breathing became less labored, he thought about the man he had seen shoot Joe Don. He had seen that man somewhere before. He knew him. He was a cold killer, that one. He was—Colfax. Colfax, that's who it was. But why had Colfax killed Joe Don? Why would Colfax be shooting at Randall Lee's boys? It didn't make any sense. It made about as much sense as a horse with wheels. Odie wheezed out a laugh. He took a deep breath and let it out slowly. He was beginning to feel better. It was quiet all round him. Soon he would get up and figure out what to do. He wondered what had become of his brother. Then he heard the unmistakable sound of a horse approaching from behind him. He clutched at twigs and dried leaves with both his hands, and he gritted his teeth.

"Oh, God, no," he whimpered. "Oh, shit, hell, God, no."

The hoofbeats stopped. The horse was practically on top of him. Odie waited for the shot.

"Oh, damn, damn, damn," he said.

Then he heard laughter. It was cruel, he thought, for someone to laugh before killing a man. Then he stopped whimpering and listened. The laugh was familiar. Odie rolled over quickly onto his back and sat up.

"You son of a bitch," he shouted.

Harlan sat on his horse as he looked down at his brother and laughed. Odie vaulted to his feet and ran at Harlan. Grabbing him by the shirt, he dragged him out of the saddle and down onto the ground. He flailed at him with his fists. Harlan continued laughing. Finally one of Odie's flailing fists found its mark and split Harlan's lower lip, splattering blood onto both brothers. Harlan's laughter stopped abruptly.

"Ow," he shouted. "You hurt me."

Odie stopped swinging and sat down in the dirt.

"Well," he said, "you was laughing at me."

"I couldn't help it," said Harlan. "You was just alaying there, shaking and crying. I never seen you so skeered. It was funny."

"Where's my horse?" said Odie.

"Hell, I don't know. I guess he's back there where we left them. I don't guess they put him on the train."

"You got your horse. Whyn't you bring mine?"

"I got my own. Whyn't you get yours?"

"I couldn't. Them two gunslingers was between me and the horses. I'd a been killed. Course that wouldn't a made no difference to you."

Somewhere deep inside of Harlan was a bit of brotherly feeling. Odie's last accusation hurt. He pouted.

"I couldn't get him," he said. "I didn't have time. I had to get out of there fast. I didn't have time."

"Shit," said Odie.

"We can go back and get him," said Harlan.

"Go back there?" said Odie. "They might be waiting for us."

"We'll sneak up to the top of the hill and take a look," said Harlan. "If the train's gone, we'll sneak on down and see if them horses is still there, and if they are, we'll get them."

Odie thought about his long run up the hill and through the woods and about how his lungs had almost burst. He rubbed a sore knee.

"All right," he said.

The Katy, having quenched its thirst, roared on down the tracks at a full twenty-five miles per hour, belching clouds of black smoke. Young Matt sat quietly beside his window seat. He knew that Luton had killed a man with the little gun he had given him, and he was proud of his part in the fight, but he was afraid that Luton would tell his mother about the gun. He knew that she wouldn't like it. So far, Luton hadn't said a word about it. He just sat there where he had been sitting all along.

Bluff Luton was thinking about Colfax. The man had come in handy in that fight by the water tank, and there had been those other times on the train. He was really a pretty good man to have around, as long as he hadn't decided the time was right for him to quit protecting Luton and to go ahead and kill him. He had said that he would tell Luton when the time had come. Still, Luton was tired of having him around. He was getting on Luton's nerves. He glanced at Emily.

"I don't know when," he said, "but I'm going to be getting off this train before we get to Henrietta. I'm worried about you and the boy getting to your destination safely. Would you tell me where I can look you up when I get there?''

"My father's name is Harold Decker," she said. "He has a rooming house in Henrietta. That's where we'll be."

"Thank you. I will be checking in on you, just to see that you're all right."

Luton excused himself and stood up to leave. He was beginning to enjoy being close to this woman, and he thought that he had to break himself away. He did not think that George Fisher would have sent more than one thug after her, and since he had tossed Ryan overboard, she and the boy would be safe until they arrived at Henrietta. He would look up Harold Decker when he got down there and make sure everything was all right. But for now he had to break away. At least start breaking away. Cut them loose. Or was he cutting himself loose? Whatever. He walked to the opposite end of the car, where Colfax sat with seemingly endless patience, like a cat at a mouse hole. He had to have some apparent purpose in taking himself away from Emily and Matt.

"Cole," he said.

Colfax tilted his head to one side so he could look up from underneath the wide hat brim.

"Let's go have a drink," said Luton.

"I thought you didn't want to have anything more to do with me until killing time," said Cole.

"Come on," said Luton, and he opened the door at the end of the car and headed on through. He didn't look back to see whether or not Colfax was following, but neither did he shut the door behind himself. Colfax heaved himself up from the bench seat and moseyed along in Luton's path. He wondered what was on the marshal's mind. Luton made his way on through the rattling line of cars until he arrived in the dining car. He found himself a table and sat down. Colfax joined him in less than a minute. They ordered brandies, Colfax with a beer chaser and Luton with a glass of water on

the side. Each man took a sip of the brandy before either one
spoke a word to the other.

"So what's on your mind?" said Colfax.

"A drink," said Luton. "That's all."

"Sure, Sarge. That's all."

"Damn it, Cole, I want a drink. I don't like to drink alone.
Unfortunately, you are the only acquaintance I've made on
this trip appropriate to have a drink with."

Colfax took another sip of the brandy and followed it with
a big swallow of beer. He looked intently at Luton.

"You want to know what I think?"

"Think what you want," said Luton. "I don't care what
you think."

"I think that you're falling in love with that woman back
there. Yes, sir. That would be just like you. Falling in love
with a divorced woman who has a child and is in trouble.
Being threatened by her former husband. You are a chival-
rous fellow. A real gentleman. So you're falling for her, but
you know that you are about to get yourself killed. If not by
me, which is most probable, by someone else the Jessup
brothers have hired. You let two of them escape back at that
watering hole. There are likely to be more of them before
this thing is over. So in true gentlemanly fashion, you have
decided to remove yourself from the lady's life."

"You don't know what the hell you're talking about," said
Luton.

"I know you, Sarge. I know you better than you think,
but I don't know you yet as well as I want to. I will, though.
Before I'm done, I will. I'll find your weak spot, your mean-
ness. It's in there somewhere."

Luton downed his drink and called for another. He didn't
like the turn the conversation had taken. He wanted to change
the subject. He was afraid that Colfax was right, and he
found it uncomfortable to be so well understood by another
human being. *Damn him*, he thought. *Why the hell did I
bring him along anyway? It ain't that bad to have to drink*

alone. He took a swallow of his water while the waiter put down his drink. Colfax still sipped on his first.

"Did you know that bunch?" asked Luton.

"What?"

"That bunch back at the water tower," said Luton. "Did you know them?"

Colfax shook his head.

"Know who they are," he said. "I wouldn't say that I know them. They're part of the recent scum of society in Denison. Those two that got away are brothers name of Bass. Illiterate, ignorant, mean."

Brothers, thought Luton. *This whole thing is happening because of my brother.* He gulped his brandy and ordered another. *The Jessup brothers. Bass brothers.* The waiter brought another brandy, and Luton took a swallow of it.

"You got any family, Cole?" he said.

"I'm alone in this world," said Colfax, "just like all the rest of you. The difference in us is that I know it. You trying to get yourself drunk?"

"You won't kill me when I'm drunk," said Luton, "and if anyone else tries, you'll protect me, because you want me for yourself—when it's killing time. Damn it, Cole, stop reading my mind."

Colfax finished his drink and ordered another round. Luton was two up on him, and that was all right as far as Colfax was concerned. Colfax did not like to be drunk. He had been really drunk only once in his life. He would have a couple of drinks, but more than that would impair his judgment and his reflexes, and a man in his profession could not afford that. He sipped on his second brandy and watched with amusement while Luton tossed his down. Luton was right, of course, he thought. He would protect the man—until killing time came around. In a way it was too bad. He was beginning to like Luton. Cole had not liked anyone in a long time. He wasn't sure if that was because he simply didn't allow himself to like them or if he hadn't found anyone who was likable. But this Luton—sooner or later, he would kill the man. It was really too bad, but Colfax was a professional and the career was everything.

It was dark outside by the time Colfax and Luton got up from the table in the dining car to make their way back to their seats in the passenger car. Luton lurched up from his chair and had to be supported by Colfax to keep from falling over. He was drunk. Cole threw one of Luton's arms over his shoulder and put his own arm around Luton's waist. In this manner, they staggered through the cars, Luton staggering from his drunkenness, Colfax from the weight and the swaying of Luton. As they stepped out onto the clattering platform between two cars, they were thrown against a safety rail. Colfax steadied them. Then Luton yelled into Colfax's ear.

"You could kill me now, Cole," he said.

"What?"

"You could kill me now. I'm just a damn drunk. You can do it with a clear conscience."

"Shut up, Sarge," said Colfax.

He managed to get Luton back to his place with Emily and Matt. They were both asleep, and the bench across from them was still empty. Colfax tossed Luton onto the empty bench, then made his own way back to his seat at the opposite end of the car. Yeah, he thought, it's a goddamned shame.

> *It must be by his death: and for my part,*
> *I know no personal cause to spurn at him. . . .*

When Bluff Luton came to his senses the next morning, his head hurt. His stomach felt somewhat insecure, and he was deeply ashamed to be in such a state in the presence of a lady and her child. He wondered where they were on their journey, but most of all, he longed for a place to hide until he felt human once more. The way he felt, he thought, Colfax might just as well have finished him off the night before.

Chapter Ten

Riding through the Cherokee Nation, Luton got a few glimpses of human beings of various types, and he thought constantly of his friend, Blue Steele, the Cherokee lawman who had allowed him to make this trip. A man with an eastern education and experience as a Shakespearean actor, Steele was not anything at all like the picture that usually formed in Luton's mind when he thought of Indians. He watched for other Cherokees, wondering if he would find them in any way similar to Steele. He was disappointed. The trip across the Cherokee Nation was for the most part like a trip through uninhabited country, until the stop at Vinita.

"Where are we?" shouted Matt.

"A town called Vinita," said Luton. "We'll probably be here for a few minutes."

"But it's all tents," said Emily.

Luton stretched his neck to see better out the window.

"I see a couple of buildings going up at the end of the street, but you're just about right. Mostly tents."

"A town made out of tents?" said Matt. "What kind of town is that?"

"Well," said Luton, "it's a tent town. That's what they call them. When the railroad goes through new territory, new towns spring up—sometimes overnight. People don't have time to build buildings, so they just put up tents. The buildings will come later.''

"Why are they in such a hurry?"

"Because they want to get our money."

"Huh?"

Luton pointed out the window to a tent not far from the tracks with a hand-painted sign propped up in front.

"You see that one right there?" he said.

"Yeah."

"Can you read the sign?"

"No."

"Well, it says, 'candy.' It's a candy store, and if the man had waited until he could get a building put up, he wouldn't be able to open his store yet. Then we wouldn't be able to go over there and get any candy. What do you think about that?"

Luton looked at Emily with a quizzing expression on his face while Matt tried to figure out how to answer the last question. Emily smiled.

"Come on, Matt," said Luton. "Let's go find out what the man's got in that tent."

As Matt jumped up and took hold of Luton's hand, Luton looked down at the boy's mother.

"You want to come along?" he asked.

They walked along the street, Matt sucking on hard candy, reading the signs on the tents which lined each side of the street. There was an attorney-at-law without even a tent. His sign was tacked on a large wooden box. He sat behind that on a smaller box. To his left was a tent offering fresh fruit juices, to his right a dentist's tent. Luton bought three cups of orange juice, and they drank them as they strolled down the street. Matt complained that his juice was sour.

"That's because of the candy," said Emily.

Luton was disappointed to find that here in the midst of the Cherokee Nation he saw so few Indians. Railroad town,

he told himself. They passed a tent with a sign hanging over
its door proclaiming it a land office. A small man stepped
forward. He was wearing baggy dark trousers dangling from
his shoulders by wide, green galluses strapped over a wrin-
kled white shirt and a slouch hat on his head. Luton imagined
that the man smiled, but he couldn't be sure because of the
shaggy mustache which completely covered the man's mouth.

"Hello, folks."

"Howdy," said Luton.

"You folks got a home lot?"

"No," said Luton, feeling suddenly embarrassed, "we're
just passing through on the train. Got a short stop."

"You could do worse than settle here," said the little man.
"I've still got a few good home lots. Be glad to show them
to you."

"No thanks, pard," said Luton. "We've got business else-
where."

Luton brushed past the little man, a bit rudely, he thought.
He hadn't realized until then just how domestic they must
appear. He felt his face flush, and he quickened his pace.

"Sarge," said Emily, "I believe you're embarrassed."

"Aw, hell," said Luton.

Even Matthew finally seemed to catch on.

"Mom, did that man think that Sarge was our daddy?"

The next stop was Muskogee, a railroad town in the Creek
Nation. Muskogee seemed a bit more settled than Vinita. It
was lunchtime, and the passengers were given a little more
time for their stop. Luton had a meal with Emily and Matt,
then managed to get himself cleaned up a bit and changed
into a fresh suit of clothes which he had packed in his valise.
Muskogee was a rowdy town, and Luton saw one fistfight in
the street and heard several shots at different times during
his short stay. He was nervous and alert in Muskogee, but as
things turned out, no one seemed to be at all interested in
either him or Emily and Matt. He lost track of Colfax during
the short stop, but when he had boarded the train once more

with Emily and Matt, there was Colfax in his usual spot at
the other end of the car. A few new passengers had joined
them, but they all appeared harmless enough, if not innocent.

"I saw lots of Indians out there," said Matt as the train
pulled out of Muskogee.

"Well," said Luton, realizing that the boy was right and
that in his nervousness at the rowdiness of the town he had
simply not noticed, "that's because we're in what they call
the Indian Territory. This part of it's called the Creek Nation,
because the Creek Indians own it. We're going through their
country."

"Will we have to fight them?"

Luton chuckled and ruffled the boy's already mussed head
of blond hair.

"No, Matt," he said, "we won't have to fight them. They
don't want to fight anybody."

"I didn't see any tepees," said Matt.

"These Indians don't live in tepees. They never did, but
nowadays they live pretty much the way we do."

"I thought they'd have feathers."

"Well, son, you live and learn," said Luton. "The man
who is watching my town for me right now is a Cherokee
Indian. He's a town marshal, just like I am."

"Really? An Indian marshal?"

"That's right."

The Katy roared on through the Creek Nation and into the
Choctaw Nation. It won't be much longer, thought Luton.
After this, a little piece of the Chickasaw Nation, the Red
River, and then Texas. Texas and the Jessups. It's almost
time. Killing time. Damn. He swore at himself for having
unconsciously used Colfax's expression. Killing time. Who
would be killed? The Jessups or Bluff Luton? Colfax? How
many? He wondered for an instant whether or not it mattered
anymore. Was it worth it? This trip, the number of men who
would die, the chance of his own death? Was it worth it after
all these years? Then he saw again the ugly face of Toad

Jessup behind the shotgun, saw the leer, saw the finger tighten on the trigger, and saw his younger brother, Bud, flung through the air by the deafening blast of the shotgun.

"It's worth it," he said.

"What?"

Luton looked at Emily, embarrassed.

"Oh, nothing, Emily," he said. "I was just thinking out loud, I guess. Excuse me."

With the trip coming nearer its end, Luton began to worry about where and when he would get off the train. If he chose a regular stop, Colfax would miss him right away and get off to follow. If he jumped off while the train was moving, he would be afoot with no way of knowing how far he would be from someplace where he could get a horse or some other means of transportation. He would have to figure out when, where, and how to get himself off the Katy, hopefully without being detected by Colfax, and then how to find his next mode of transportation. Colfax was going to be a problem. He knew that. There had already been times when he had lost sight of Colfax, but Colfax had seemed to know just where he had been. The man was uncanny, clever, mysterious. But he was just a man. Any man could be beaten. Any man could be outsmarted. But that could work both ways, and Luton reminded himself once again that the job at Riddle had been too easy for too long. Being realistic about it all, he realized that one of his options was really no option at all. He did not intend to jump off a moving train—not at his age and in his present out-of-shape condition.

Brad Collins was half Cherokee and half white, neither of which meant much of anything to him. Culturally he was a border ruffian who usually made his money by selling whiskey illegally in the Indian Nations. When things had become too hot for him in the Cherokee Nation, he had moved south to the Choctaw Nation. The railroad through Indian Territory had been a boon to Brad Collins, for it brought along in its wake so many of his type that he was able more easily to

blend in. It took the attention of the law enforcement officers
off him just a bit. Most of the Indians, and certainly the
governments of the Indian Nations, had been strongly op-
posed to the coming of railroads for precisely the reasons
that Collins welcomed them. On this particular day in Brad
Collin's twenty-sixth year of life, he was especially pleased
that the railroads had come. He was nearly broke, and he
needed some capital to finance his next whiskey run. He had
gathered about him a gang of railroad-terminus-town types—
broke, desperate, shiftless, rowdy, and thoroughly amoral.
Carefully selected, they were either just cowardly enough to
be bullied and bossed by Collins, or just stupid enough to
need his guidance. There was Cherokee Jake, who might or
might not have been part Cherokee. There was Six-toes, who
really did have six toes on each foot. There was Black Bob
and Jinks and Skeeter. These men were all men who had left
behind them along with cloudy pasts the names their mothers
had given them at birth. Then there was the Kid, who either
by the grace of God or the luck of the addle-brained, had
lasted into his late teen years after having been abandoned
by some unknown woman with no motherly instincts. He
had never had a name to leave behind. This was the Brad
Collins Gang.

They had boarded the train one or two at a time at different
sites—Muskogee, Checotah, Atoka—so as not to call attention to themselves, and they carried their pistols concealed
under loose-fitting jackets. Brad Collins sat across the aisle
from Oliver Colfax. Just behind Sergeant Bluff Luton was
Cherokee Jake. The others rode in other cars. Brad Collins
had a plan, and he thought that it was a good one. His men
were not bright, but they didn't need to be. He did all the
thinking for them. All they had to do was remember what he
had told them and follow his instructions, and they were
capable of that. It was going to work. Up ahead was a steep
grade that would slow the train down. On the west side of
the tracks were the foothills of the Arbuckle Mountains, but
on the opposite side was a wide and flat expanse of prairie.

It was a good spot to stop the train, Collins had figured, and Black Bob knew just the right time to move. Soon Black Bob would climb up over the wood car, which was just behind the engine, and slip up behind the engineer and fireman, throwing down on them with his ancient Navy Colt. He would order them to stop the train. When Collins and the others felt the train slowing for a stop, they would jump up from their seats in their respective cars and cover all the passengers. It was just about foolproof and, Collins thought, it had to be, for he was working with fools.

Collins braced himself as he felt the train begin to slow down for the grade. Soon it became evident that it was slowing more than the climb would explain. He jerked out his pistol and stepped into the aisle, taking care to aim at the dangerous-looking man across the aisle. An instant behind him, Cherokee Jake stood at the other end of the car, gun in hand. Collins looked hard at Colfax.

"Take out that pistol and lay it on the floor," he said.

Colfax did as he was told.

"Everybody," said Collins, "this is a holdup. I'm Brad Collins. Put your hands up in the air. You do as I say, and nobody gets hurt."

Collins looked back at Colfax, the Colt on the floor at his feet.

"You move over here," he said.

Colfax moved to the seat Collins had vacated.

"Anybody else on this car carrying any weapons?" said Collins.

"This guy's got a gun," said Cherokee Jake.

"Get it."

Jake reached down and removed Luton's Starr from its holster. Luton tensed, but he didn't make a move to stop Jake. *A holdup?* he thought. *Or are they after me? If I live through this I've got to get off this train. Everybody in the country seems to know I'm on it, and this is the second attack on the train. Somebody innocent could get killed because of me*. He watched as Cherokee Jake stuck the Starr in the waistband of his trousers. By this time the train was almost stopped, and it came to a complete stop with a sudden lurch.

"All right," said Collins, "everybody, slow and easy. Get off the train. Keep your hands up where we can see them."

The passengers disembarked and were herded together out onto the flatland to the east of the tracks. The rest of the gang brought the passengers and the crew from the other cars to join them.

"Kid," said Collins, "fill up that sack. Jake, you come with me. The rest of you just stand here and keep everybody calm."

Collins led the way to the freight car with Cherokee Jake following, and while Six-toes, Black Bob, and Jinks held their guns on the crowd, the Kid moved around from one passenger to another with his canvas bag held wide open.

"Fill it up," he said. "Fill it up."

He met with no resistance. As Luton emptied his pockets and dropped their contents into the bag, he thought about the tiny derringer in his coat pocket. For an instant he thought about dropping it into the bag, but it occurred to him that if he pulled the pistol out of his pocket, the move might easily be misinterpreted. He left it there and hoped that the Kid wouldn't frisk him and find it. It was of no use anyway. Both shots had been fired, and Luton had no .41 shells to fit it. The Starr, which was now tucked in the britches of Cherokee Jake, was a .44, as was his Winchester, so the only ammunition Luton packed was .44. He still considered the possibility that these men were after the money offered for him by the Jessups. Perhaps they were taking the opportunity to get double for their effort by killing him for the Jessup reward and robbing the train at the same time. If so, he wondered, when would they make their move on him? The Kid did not pause at Luton after Luton had emptied his pockets of everything but the derringer. He just moved on to Emily, who dumped the contents of her purse into the bag. Soon Collins and Cherokee Jake returned. Jake was carrying a bag similar to the one the Kid had.

"You done here?" said Collins.

"Cleaned 'em out," said the Kid with a big grin on his baby face.

"Damn it," said Collins, "where the hell is Skeeter?"

Just then a rider leading six saddled horses appeared from around the engine.

"Let's go," said Collins. "Thank you, folks. We appreciate it."

The bandits mounted up and rode toward the engine, then cut across to the west side of the tracks. As soon as the last rider had disappeared around the engine, Luton bolted for the passenger car in which he had been riding. Colfax was close behind him. Inside the car, Luton reached for his blanket roll and pulled out the Winchester which he had stashed in there. Then he ran back outside. Colfax found his Colt on the floor at the other end of the car and again was close behind. While Luton ran for the tracks in front of the train, Colfax climbed to the top of the passenger car. Two riders were still in sight up ahead. The other five had already disappeared around a bend and were covered by the wooded hillside to the west of the tracks. Colfax fired twice, both shots missing their marks. The distance was too great for any real accuracy from the Colt.

"Goddamn it," he said.

Up beside the engine, Luton rested his right arm on top of the massive cowcatcher, took careful aim, and fired. Skeeter, the farthest ahead of the two riders, threw his arms up over his head and toppled backward out of the saddle just as his horse disappeared around the bend. Luton cranked the Winchester quickly, resumed his position, and fired again. Jinks jerked, leaned forward across his animal's neck, and kept riding. Luton ran down the tracks after them. Colfax climbed down off the passenger car and followed. He caught up with Luton, standing beside the body of Skeeter, just as Luton was nudging the body with the toe of his boot.

"Dead?" said Colfax.

"Yeah. Come on."

They trotted on down the tracks and around the bend, where they found Jinks. A horse was milling nervously around beside the tracks. Colfax moved to the body to check it while Luton eased up on the nervous horse.

"This one's dead, too," said Colfax. "Good shooting."

"They were easy shots with a rifle," said Luton. He gathered the reins up around the horse's neck and put a foot in a stirrup.

"What the hell are you doing?" said Colfax.

"I'm going to see if I can catch that other horse so we can follow those bastards."

Colfax thumbed back the hammer on his Colt and aimed it at Luton's back.

"I'll catch it," he said. "You wait for me back at the train."

Luton hesitated, his foot still in the stirrup. He looked over his shoulder at Colfax. There was no way he could swing the Winchester into play before Colfax could get off his shot. He wondered whether or not Colfax would actually kill him right then and there if he ignored the order, and swung up into the saddle. He didn't think so, but then, it didn't seem worth the chance to find out. He eased his foot out of the stirrup and dropped the reins.

"Suit yourself," he said, "but hurry up about it. I don't relish finishing out this trip without money in my pockets."

Colfax moved to take the horse.

"We'll get it back," he said.

As Colfax rode around the bend and out of sight, Luton walked back to the train. The conductor was starting to herd the passengers back on board, and the engineer had climbed back into the cab. Luton walked over to Emily.

"Don't worry," he said. "We're going after them. We'll get back your money."

"I don't think you should," said Emily. "It's too dangerous."

"Look," he said, "they left me broke, too, and I need my money. Besides, don't forget, chasing outlaws is my line of work."

"Get on board, folks," shouted the conductor.

"Go ahead, Emily," said Luton. "I'll see you again. Go on."

Colfax rode up, leading the other horse. He paused beside the engine.

"Don't get up too much steam," he shouted to the engineer.

"Why not?"

"They've blocked the tracks up ahead."

"Damn."

The engineer climbed back out of the cab and walked toward the conductor, who was still trying to get all the passengers back on board as Colfax walked the horses over to where Luton stood.

"Steve," said the engineer, "the tracks are blocked up ahead. Tell everyone we're just going to ease on up there. Then we'll need all the help we can get to clear them."

He turned to go back to the engine.

"Shit," said Steve.

Luton mounted the horse which Colfax was leading and turned it around.

"Come on," he said.

Brad Collins had led his gang a short way down the tracks beyond the barrier which they had created to block the tracks, then turned west into a dry creekbed which would lead them on into the Arbuckle Mountains. He had heard the sound of the four shots behind him, and he had noticed that two of his men were missing. He was glad to note that neither of the two had been carrying the bags which contained the stolen loot. He realized also that there were now two loose horses back near the site of the holdup and that there was at least the possibility of pursuit by two men. He thought of the two men who rode at opposite ends of the same passenger car,

the car which he himself had been on, who had both guns
and the appearance of gunfighters. They were probably the
ones who had shot Skeeter and Jinks. One must have a pistol,
the other a rifle. They could have then rounded up the slain
men's horses. He had to figure out how to deal with this new
development, this unforeseen turn of events. It had never
entered his mind that someone from the train would wind up
mounted on horses from his gang. He rode as hard as the
terrain would allow, the four remaining members of his gang
following close behind, and he considered his dilemma,
glancing often over his shoulder in anticipation of possible
pursuit.

Luton pulled up his mount at the side of the tracks. He
was studying the ground off to his right.

"They went off here," he said. "Headed up that draw."

"It won't be hard to track them," said Colfax.

"No," said Luton, "but it ain't going to be easy to sneak
up on 'em either. Trees and brush are pretty thick up through
there."

"I don't see any other way."

"Chances are good they heard those shots," said Luton.
"Probably miss their two buddies by now. They could be
watching over their shoulders, looking to be followed. Could
even be laying an ambush."

"So what do we do, Sarge?"

"I don't know. Follow them slow and easy for a ways, I
guess. See what we can think of along the way."

Luton led the way into the creekbed, going slowly, watching the tracks, and looking carefully ahead. It was ironic, he
thought, that he was here pursuing train robbers in the Choctaw Nation with a man who had been hired to kill him. *Life
sometimes deals a man a strange hand. He's riding at my
back, too. Funny, the way I trust the son of a bitch.*

Brad Collins urged his mount up onto the crest of a hill
where the ground suddenly leveled off for twenty yards or

so, the hills rising on up beyond that. He rode over to one side to allow the others to achieve the rise with him, and as they did so, he halted them.

"Hold up right here," he said.

"What is it, Brad?" asked Cherokee Jake.

"I'm afraid we might be followed."

"You said wouldn't nobody follow us up here," said Six-toes.

"I didn't think there'd be anyone with a horse," said Collins. "Now shut up and listen to me, all of you. As we was riding off, there was four shots. Sounded like two pistol shots and two rifle shots. Skeeter and Jinks fell behind, and they ain't caught up with us yet. Now what does that make you think?"

"Somebody got 'em," said the Kid.

"Yeah," said Collins, "and if somebody got 'em, then that same somebody could have got their horses and could be following us."

"Then what are we stopping for?" said Six-toes. "Why ain't we getting out of here? Huh?"

"Because if I'm right, then there's only just two of them. Right? Skeeter and Jinks. Two horses. One pistol and one rifle. Just two of them. We wait right here and pick them off as they come up the hill."

"But what if they ain't coming?" said the Kid. "How long do we wait?"

"We'll wait, but we'll find out if they're really coming or not. Six-toes, I want you to ride back down the trail. Real easy. Find out if they're down there and if it's two of them like I think, and get back up here and tell us. Go on."

Six-toes turned his horse around and started to ease back down the trail. Collins watched him go, thinking that what would likely happen would be that Six-toes would come upon their pursuers and get himself killed, but that was all right with Collins. There would be one less to split with. The shares were getting bigger with each downed outlaw. In addition, Six-toes might possibly get one or both of the pur-

suers, and even if he didn't, which was more likely, Collins
and the others waiting at the top of the hill would hear the
gunshots and have some idea how far behind the two were.
Then they could either set up the ambush in earnest or ride
on and evade the pursuit.

"Climb on down, boys," he said. "We've got a little wait."

Emily Fisher stood with Matt at her side along the railroad
tracks, watching the able-bodied male passengers help the
train crew clear the tracks of a large pile of logs and brush.
She had left her wrap on the train and was beginning to feel
a chill in the air.

"Come on, Matt," she said, and as she turned, she saw
five mounted and uniformed riders approaching from the
north.

"Mom," said Matt. "Look. Indians."

The riders were, indeed, Indians. The Choctaw Nation,
like its neighboring nations, known to the world collectively
as "the Five Civilized Tribes," had a mounted national police force called the Light Horse. The five riders were rep-
resentatives of that group. Suddenly finding their path
blocked by a woman and child, they reined in their mounts.
The man in the lead touched the brim of his hat as he spoke
to Emily.

"Howdy, ma'am," he said. "Can you tell us what's going
on here?"

Emily looked stunned.

"Excuse me," said the rider. "We're members of the national police force. The Light Horse. Has there been some
trouble here?"

"Yes," said Emily, "the train was robbed, and the tracks
ahead are blocked. The men are trying to get them cleared.
It was someone named Collins, I think."

"Brad Collins," said the rider. "Thank you, ma'am."

Emily took Matt by the hand and walked him past the
riders and back to the passenger car. The Light Horsemen
rode on ahead to where the tracks were blocked. The con-

ductor spotted them first and stepped away from the work crew.

"I'm glad to see you," he said. "We've just been held up."

"Anyone hurt?"

"No. Well, yeah. Two of the outlaws."

He pointed across the tracks to a spot where the bodies of Skeeter and Jinks had been dragged and laid out side by side. The leader of the Light Horse rode over to take a look. He called back to his fellow policemen.

"It's Skeeter and Jinks," he said. "Sure ain't no loss."

He climbed down out of the saddle and walked back to the conductor.

"Who got them?" he asked.

"Two passengers. They took the outlaws' horses and went after the rest of the gang."

"How many in the gang?"

"Seven, I think. Be five left."

"Two men riding after five outlaws? That's pretty damn foolish."

"Maybe," said the train man. "These two looked tough to me. They got the look of gunfighters."

"Well, I hope they are, for their sakes. We'll go after them anyhow. You folks got things under control here?"

"Yeah. It'll take us awhile to get the tracks clear, but there's nothing you can do to help. We're all right. Go on after those outlaws."

The policeman climbed back into his saddle and said something in Choctaw, then started riding south along the tracks. The others followed him.

Chapter Eleven

Bluff Luton stopped his horse abruptly in the middle of the dry wash leading up into the Arbuckles. He made no gesture, no sound to indicate why he had done so. Colfax stopped behind him. He sat and watched Luton. Something, he knew, had caused Luton to haul up like that. Luton was an old lawman, a manhunter, and a damn good one. The fact that he was still alive was a testimonial to his success. He might have heard something, but Colfax doubted that. He would have heard it, too, probably. If he had seen something, there would have been some immediate action. No, Colfax thought, it's an instinct. He had had them himself in the past, and he respected them. He would wait until Luton told him something or made some kind of move. Then he saw Luton's right hand slowly raise and gesture toward the right side of the draw repeatedly. Colfax eased himself out of the saddle, hauled out his Colt, and crept toward the bushes to the right. Luton went off on the other side with the Winchester. Soon Colfax heard what had stopped Luton.

It sounded like a horse coming down the draw toward them. Colfax eased back the hammer on his Colt. The horse was getting closer, and now he could tell that it was just one horse. Six-toes, mounted on his gray, appeared almost at

91

once. He jerked his reins in surprise at the two loose horses standing in his way.

"What the hell?" he said.

Luton's voice sounded from the brush to Six-toes's right. "Throw down your gun."

Six-toes reached for his pistol and fired a wild shot into the brush, and an instant later a slug from Colfax's Colt tore through his neck. Six-toes jerked, slumped, and slowly slid from the saddle. Colfax stepped out into the draw, where he was soon joined by Luton.

"There's still four of them up ahead," said Colfax.

"Yeah," said Luton, "and now they know for sure that we're down here. More than likely, they'll have laid an ambush. Be waiting for us."

"Well, we sure don't want to ride into it. Any suggestions?"

Luton scratched his head and looked at the grotesque remains of Six-toes lying twisted in the dry creekbed. It was just a train robbery, after all, he thought.

"Yeah," he said, "probably the same thing you're thinking about."

Brad Collins was already getting nervous when he heard the shots. In spite of himself, he flinched at the sound. Then he cocked his six-gun. At the sound of the clicks of the double-action handgun, Black Bob and Cherokee Jake also thumbed theirs back.

"Two shots," said the Kid. "He got them."

"Shut up, Kid," said Collins.

"But he got them, didn't he?"

"They got him."

"Two shots," said the Kid. "You said two men coming. How you know he didn't get them?"

"Them two shots was from two different guns, Kid," said Collins. "They got him. Now shut up and watch for them."

Captain Billie led his Choctaw Light Horsemen down the railroad tracks until he found the spot where several horses

had turned off to the west and headed up a dry wash. He
looked over his shoulder and said something in Choctaw
to his men, then led them up into the wash. There were
five outlaws up there somewhere, being pursued by two
railroad passengers. Billie didn't know who the passengers
were, but he did know that the leader of the outlaws was
Brad Collins, a dangerous man. He wished that the two
men had stayed with the train. The Light Horse could handle the situation just fine, but two amateurs in the way
could complicate matters some. The train man he had
talked to had said that the two had the look of gunmen.
Well, Captain Billie certainly hoped that they lived up to
their looks, for their own sakes. Brad Collins was bad,
and Billie had a fair idea who the others with him would
be. Skeeter and Jinks were dead back at the tracks. Up
ahead still with Collins were probably Six-toes, Black Bob,
Cherokee Jake, and the Kid. He knew them all by sight,
by reputation, and by the handles they chose to go by. No
one knew their names.

Captain Billie's mind was brought back to the present
abruptly when he spied three horses in the path ahead and
down at their feet what appeared to be a body.

"Ho," he said, drawing back the reins to stop his horse.
He barked out a quick command in the Choctaw language,
and all the policemen dismounted and pulled out their pistols. Leading their horses, they followed Captain Billie cautiously up the draw to the spot where the animals and the
body awaited their attention.

"Six-toes," said Captain Billie.

Luton and Colfax had abandoned their horses back where
Six-toes lay and had moved, one to each side of the draw,
into the woods to work their way up to the top of the hill.
They had figured that the outlaws might be there waiting for
them. Luton had said that when he was in position, he would
call out to the outlaws to surrender. They would try to take
them back alive for the authorities to deal with. If the outlaws

insisted on making a fight out of it, so be it, but Colfax was to wait for Luton's offer to the outlaws before making any move.

At the top of the hill, the Kid was getting more nervous. Collins was afraid that if their pursuers didn't show up soon, he would have to knock the Kid in the head to keep him still and quiet. Then he heard someone call out his name from the woods.

"Brad Collins."

Collins flinched and turned his head in the direction of the sound of the voice, but before he could holler out, the Kid stood up from behind the rock where he had been secreted and sent a wild shot into the brush. A Colt barked from off in the opposite direction and sent the Kid sprawling backward in the dirt. Then everyone was shooting. Collins thought about the money. One sack was on the ground beside the Kid. The other was still hanging from the saddle of Cherokee Jake. He also thought about his hide, and he decided that he wanted to get away. To hell with the others. He moved toward the body of the Kid, and a shot threw dirt into his face. He moved back again. Just then Black Bob screamed and stood up, clutching at his face, and another shot caught him in the chest and dropped him. Collins scampered behind some rocks, moving west along the ridge. Back at the ambush site, Cherokee Jake saw that Collins was deserting him. He was the only one left. He shouted at Collins.

"Brad. Brad, come back here, you son of a bitch."

Collins kept scampering, and Jake fired a shot after him. It went wide. Jake stood to get a better shot, and Colfax hit him between the shoulder blades with a slug from his Colt. Collins had worked his way along the ridge a good distance by then, and he dove headlong down the hillside into the thicket. The silence was as sudden as the noise had been just a few short minutes earlier.

Captain Billie and the Light Horse heard the shots. It would be foolish to go charging up the draw and right into the middle of all that without knowing the situation. Captain Billie directed his men to the sides of the draw and into the bushes. He tried to think of a good strategy, but the firing stopped almost as soon as it had begun. Whatever had happened up there, it was over. But who had won? He would still have to work his men cautiously up to the top of the hill. There might be two dead railroad passengers and four live outlaws up there. He decided to work his force on up to the top, half on each side of the creekbed just at the edge of the woods. He gave the orders, and they started.

Luton and Colfax stepped out onto the flat at the top of the rise and examined the bodies. All three were dead. The two money sacks were both there, as were all the horses.

"One got away," said Colfax.

"Yeah," said Luton, "I think it was Collins. To hell with him. At least he got away empty-handed."

Luton rolled over the body of Cherokee Jake and found his Starr still there in the outlaw's waistband. He pulled it out, hefted it a couple of times, and shoved it back into its holster, which had been hanging empty on his hip. He felt much better. Then he turned to Colfax.

"You'll never find a better place or time," he said.

Colfax faced Luton and squinted. He tugged at his belt, then turned his back on Luton and started to walk toward the outlaws' horses.

"I ain't ready," he said.

Luton made a quick decision, took two long steps after Colfax, and swung the Winchester hard, smashing the stock against the back of Colfax's head. Colfax dropped like a grain sack. Luton nudged him with his foot. Colfax was out cold—or worse. Luton knelt beside him to check and found that he was still alive. *Good,* he thought. *I didn't want to kill him. Not like that.* He picked up the money sack from beside the body of the Kid, mounted the horse that had been ridden by Cherokee Jake, with the other sack still hanging on its saddle, and rode off along the ridge in the same direction Brad Collins had gone before he had dived down the hill.

Easing his way up the draw, Captain Billie heard a violent rustling of brush to his back. It was not near. It sounded as if it was deeper in the woods. He held up his hand in a gesture to his men to halt, and he listened. It sounded like someone in a hurry to get down the hill, but whoever it was had taken the hard way—through the woods rather than down the dry creekbed. Billie turned to the man nearest him and whispered an order. The man turned to the man behind him, said something, and the two of them reversed their course and started down the draw. Captain Billie decided to move a little faster. He hurried the remainder of his small posse on up to the top of the hill, where he found nothing but bodies. Strange, he thought. There ought to be someone left alive. He thought about the noise in the woods as he looked over the bodies. He recognized the Kid, Cherokee Jake, and Black Bob. Then he found that the fourth body was alive, and that it was a stranger. It could be an unidentified outlaw or it could be one of the passengers. The man had no gun. All the outlaws' guns were with their bodies. There was no sign of Brad Collins, and there were only three horses. There was also no sign of the other passenger, if this one was one of the two. It was a puzzle, but he would try to work it out later. He sent a man down the draw to get their horses and the three loose ones they had found there. They would load up the bodies and the wounded man and go back to the train. There at least they could ascertain the identity of the wounded man.

Brad Collins fought his way frantically through the thick underbrush of the wooded hillside. As he rushed headlong downward, branches lashed at his face, and he flailed wildly at them with his arms. Thoughts darted spastically through his brain. *I should have killed them two gunfighters on the train.* He tripped and rolled, lacerating a knee on a rock which jutted out of the earth. *Damn it.* He scampered to his feet again, but his forward motion caused him to fall on his face. *Damn. Killed them all.* He collided with a tree trunk, shoved himself away from it, and raced on. *Got to start all over now. All over. Next time, get some guys with some brains. Damn gunfighters.* A branch slapped him in the face, and he swatted at it, spinning all the way around and losing his balance. He fell backward and rolled into a ditch. He was out of the woods. He was on his back and looking up at two uniformed Indians, each holding a pistol pointed at his head.

Bluff Luton rode along the ridge until he found a spot that looked as if he could ride down through without too much trouble. The ridge trail had taken him west, but he imagined that the railroad tracks followed the Arbuckle foothills anyhow, so that he had not really gone too far out of his way. It was steep and a little tricky, not nearly so easy to negotiate as the dry wash had been, but he managed to get to the bottom. He was south and west of where he had left Colfax and the bodies of the bandits. He found the railroad tracks without any trouble, and he turned north. He would return the money sacks to the train and then ride out on his own. He rode easy along the side of the tracks, and as he rode, he opened one of the sacks and counted out his own money. He stuffed the money into his pockets and looked up just as he was about to round a bend. Up ahead were two uniformed Indians, national police, he imagined, holding guns on a man. He couldn't see well enough to tell who the man was. He halted the horse and watched. The two policemen gestured with their guns, and the man walked ahead of them. Luton eased his mount forward to keep an eye on the proceedings. Soon the prisoner at the urging of his captors turned west and walked into the trees. Luton rode on ahead carefully until he reached the spot where they had turned off. He recognized it as the same dry creekbed he had ridden up earlier with Colfax. So the police were up there. Good, he thought. Maybe that's Collins they've got. He kicked the horse in the sides and hurried on past the wash and on toward the train. He hoped it would still be there.

Luton reached the train just as the men were clearing the last of the rubble off the tracks. He singled out the conductor.

"We caught up with them," he said. "Here's all the stolen money. See that it gets back to the rightful owners."

"Where's the other fellow?"

"He's still up there on the hill where we shot it out. Indian police are up there, too. They'll get it all straightened out. I'll be leaving the train here."

Luton handed the bags to the conductor.

"No one got away with anything," he said.

"Thanks, mister. We sure are obliged to you for this. And to your friend."

Luton rode on down to the passenger car in which he had been riding and dismounted. Emily met him at the door with little Matt crowding around her skirts.

"Hi, Sarge," said Matt.

"Hi there, Matt."

"Are you all right?" said Emily.

"Oh, yeah, I'm fine. They've all been killed or captured. Colfax and the Indian police are still up there. I just returned all the stolen money to the conductor, and he'll be getting what's yours back to you. I'm leaving now, Emily. Like I said before, I'll look you up in Texas."

"Thank you for everything you've done for us," said Emily.

"It wasn't nothing," he said, and he rubbed the top of Matt's head. "You look after your mother, boy."

"All right," said Matt.

Luton picked up his blanket roll and valise, stepped down off the car, tied them on behind the saddle, and mounted Cherokee Jake's horse again. He couldn't follow the tracks. He would be likely to meet up with the police, who would surely want to question him, and that would waste time. He might even meet up with Colfax. He couldn't head west into the Arbuckles. He would have to swing around to the east across the flatland for a while, then head back south to the river. He had gotten Colfax off his back, at least for a while.

Chapter Twelve

Luton felt a little sorry for what he had done to Colfax. It wasn't his style to hit a man from behind, but he had things to do—important things, things that had waited too many years. Luton knew that this was going to be his last chance, and he couldn't afford to let Colfax, or anyone else for that matter, interfere with it. Colfax would recover. He'd be all right, and Luton was certain that he'd be seeing the man again sometime, someplace. But for now Colfax wasn't a problem, and Luton had to get his mind back to present problems. How to get across the river and down into Texas undetected, how to locate the Jessups and how to get at them, and how to stay alive while doing all that—those were the immediate considerations. His brother's features loomed into his mind, and he tried to fight off the haunting image by studying the landscape and trying to figure out his route to the Red River.

He noticed that his limbs were sore. He was sore all over. He tried to let his body relax and roll with the rhythms of the horse, but it didn't help much. He was in pain. *I've gotten old*, he thought. *Old and soft. Damn it.* He forced his mind back to his plans. He would find a Red River crossing away from the railroad tracks, then he would ride to Henrietta to

make sure that Emily and Matt had made it safely to her
father. What was his name? Decker. That was it. Harold
Decker. That done, he would try to find Will Milam. He
would have to do these things without being noticed, if possible. It would be best to arrive at Henrietta under cover of
darkness. Then when he had found Will, Will could provide
him with information on the Jessups. They were probably to
be found at Will's former ranch, but Luton didn't know where
that was. Milam had acquired, built up, and lost his ranch
all since Luton had left Texas. He had no idea how much
change to expect. He would be in unfamiliar country—
country which had once been familiar to him, but that had
been too many years ago. Not knowing what the setup would
be, he couldn't plan any farther ahead than that. He would
have to figure out just how to go after the Jessups after he
had met and talked with Will Milam. Damn, his bones and
muscles ached. Too much action lately, and too little for too
many years.

When Oliver Colfax regained consciousness, the first thing
he was aware of was a tremendous throbbing pain in his
head. The pain was accompanied by an overwhelming fuzzy-
minded confusion. He reached up to his head and felt a wet
rag, and he rubbed at the pain through the rag. Then he
remembered turning his back on Luton. *Damn,* he thought,
*I wouldn't ever have believed it of him. I didn't give the man
enough credit.* It was almost funny, but Colfax didn't laugh.
His head hurt too badly. He slowly opened his eyes and discovered himself to be laid out on a bench seat in a railroad
car. He started to sit up, groaned, and lay back down. Then
he heard a voice. It sounded, he thought, small, like a
woman.

"Captain Billie."

Colfax saw Emily Fisher standing over him, and in answer
to the voice, an Indian wearing a uniform came walking down
the aisle.

"Captain Billie, he's awake."

Billie sat down across from Colfax.

"How you feeling?" he said.

"Like hell," said Colfax.

"We got all the loot back from the train robbers, thanks to you and Mr. Luton," said Billie, "and we caught Collins. You two got all the rest of them. I want to thank you for your help."

Colfax groaned.

"I got to ask you a couple of questions."

"Go ahead," said Colfax. "Shoot."

"Well," said Billie, "I know that Luton rode back down here to deliver the money, but I don't know what happened to you. Luton told Mrs. Fisher here that you were still up on the hill with the outlaws. Can you tell me what happened?"

Colfax groaned again as he sat up. He took the rag in his hands and mopped his head with it. If he told the policeman what had happened, that Luton had bashed him in the head when his back was turned, the Light Horse would go after Luton. They might catch him. If he resisted, they might kill him. Colfax decided that the Choctaw police didn't need to know just exactly what had occurred on the hill.

"Well," he said, "he was right. He brought back the loot and I stayed up on the hill."

"What happened to you then?" said Captain Billie.

"I don't know for sure. There was three dead outlaws on the ground, and one had escaped. I figured that he had run off for good, so I wasn't too worried about him, but then somebody came up behind me and conked me."

Colfax chuckled to himself. He hadn't even lied to the man. Captain Billie stood up.

"It must have been Collins," he said. "Everyone else is accounted for. Do you know why Luton took off on horseback?"

"No."

"He had planned to leave the train soon," Emily said. "He told me."

"Well, technically he's riding a stolen horse," said Billie, "but under the circumstances, I don't think we'll worry about that. Mr. Colfax, thank you again. I guess we'll let this train get to rolling."

Captain Billie got off the train and soon the engine started chugging.

So, thought Colfax, *he took off on horseback. He told the woman he was going to leave the train. Trying to give me the slip. That's all right. I know where he's headed, so I'll just stick right here and look him up in Texas.*

Luton rode most of the rest of that day, generally heading southeast. The sun was just about to disappear for the night when he spotted a small frame house. There was a man in front of the house working at something. The distance was yet too great for Luton to tell what it was. He urged the horse on toward the house. Soon he could see that the man was Indian, and that he had been busy sharpening a hoe. He was no longer busy, though, having spotted Luton's approach. He stood here, hoe in hand, waiting. Luton rode up into the yard.

"Howdy," he said.

"Howdy."

"I'm traveling to Texas," said Luton. "I'm hungry, and so is this horse. Can you help us out? I can pay."

"Climb on down, mister. I don't sell food and water, but you're welcome to it here. You can take care of your horse over here. Then we'll go in."

An Indian woman's face appeared in the doorway to the house, and the man said something to her in the Choctaw language. She disappeared back into the house. The man took Luton's horse by the reins and led him to a watering trough back behind the house.

"You got a name?" he said.

"Luton. Bluff Luton. My friends call me 'Sarge.' "

"Well, Sarge, my friends call me 'Tubby.' That don't mean I'm fat. It's just short for my long Indian name."

Tubby pulled the horse away from the water.

"That's enough for now," he said. He walked him over to a stack of hay bales and broke the end off one.

"Here you go," he said. He turned to Luton. "Ain't got no oats just now."

"He'll be just fine with that," said Luton.

"Come on," said Tubby. "Let's go in."

Tubby led Luton into the house through a back door and offered him a chair at the kitchen table. Luton sat down, and the Indian woman he had seen at the front door poured him a cup of coffee and placed the cup before him at the table.

"Thank you," said Luton.

The woman smiled, and Tubby spoke to her in Choctaw. Then he sat down across the table from Luton.

"She don't speak no English," he said. "But she'll feed you good."

"Oh, I see. Well, would you please tell her for me that I appreciate it very much? Tell her thank you."

Again Tubby spoke to his wife in their native tongue. She smiled and nodded her head at Luton and continued her work. The coffee was good and strong, made by boiling grounds in a pot of water. It was the kind of coffee Luton referred to as "cowboy coffee," although at one point in the evening Tubby called it "Indian coffee" and apologized for the free-floating grounds. Luton suggested that the grounds gave it substance, and said that it was very good. Tubby must have translated that into Choctaw for his wife, for he said something to her that made her giggle. The meal was fine, too. Luton particularly liked the bean bread, and he was a little ashamed of himself for eating so much. When the meal was finished, Tubby spoke to Luton.

"You got a long ride ahead of you yet, Sarge," he said. "It's night and you need a place to sleep. You stay here tonight and get started in the morning."

"I wouldn't want to put you out anymore," said Luton.

"No bother," said Tubby. "You want to ride all night?"

"Well, no."

"Then it's settled."

* * *

The following morning, Luton saddled his horse and re-packed his blanket roll and valise. He was pleased that the horse wore a saddle holster for the Winchester. He had been fed a hearty breakfast by Mrs. Tubby, and had just finished strapping the blanket roll down when Tubby came walking up.

"Can you tell me where I can find a good river crossing near here?" Luton asked the Choctaw.

"Best place is Colbert's Ferry," said Tubby. "Where the railroad crosses."

"I'd rather not cross there."

Tubby shot Luton a quick glance, then looked back down at the ground.

"Well," he said, "there is another place not far from here. It's kind of tricky, but I could show you."

"I'd appreciate it," said Luton, "if it's not too much trouble."

While Tubby went back inside the house to tell his wife where he was going, Luton saddled Tubby's mare for him. He decided that he would give the man some money when they reached the river crossing. He wouldn't accept pay for his hospitality, but now he would be serving as a guide. That would be different, and this time Luton would insist. He thought about Blue Steele again, and then he thought about Tubby. These Indians were fine people, he thought. He hadn't really known any Indians before he met Steele, so Tubby was really only the second. Growing up in Texas, he had heard only the worst, and he realized that he was feeling a pang of guilt about his native state. Yes, he would definitely insist on paying Tubby for the trip to the river crossing. *You live and learn,* he told himself. *A man's never too old to learn something new. No, sir.*

Riding on the train next to the empty spot where Luton had been, Emily realized how much she missed the man. He had been a great help to her, had in fact saved her from

God knows what. Ryan might actually have been able to force her and Matt to return to Boston had Luton not been there to help. She chuckled at the thought of Ryan flailing his arms as he flew through the air in his unexpected departure from the train. She put an arm around Matt, who was asleep beside her, and she wondered if they would ever see Luton again. He had said he would look her up in Texas. Yet she wondered. Something was wrong that he had not told her about, and she had not asked. It was really none of her business. But there was something. She could sense it, and she felt that somehow that strange man Colfax had something to do with it.

Chapter Thirteen

Luton got across the river and into Texas without any trouble. *Funny*, he thought, *it ain't any distance at all across that river, but the feeling is sure different. I'm back in Texas, all right*. He rode up through the trees that lined the riverbank and on out onto the flat prairie.

"Texas," he said out loud, talking to the horse or to himself. "Worse than that. North Texas."

He swung down out of the saddle and let the reins trail on the ground while he took in the landscape. There was something in it that didn't seem familiar, something that seemed somewhat out of place. He couldn't quite put his finger on it, but it was there. He strolled over to a scruffy little tree that stood alone and forlorn. He couldn't lean on it for the long thorns. Then it came to him. Mesquites. Those damned imported mesquite trees. He had seen them years ago in south Texas, but when he had headed north they hadn't been in evidence. Damn things have spread all the way up here.

He knew that he was northeast of Sherman. Had he stayed on the train, he would have crossed the Red at Colbert's Ferry and gone almost directly south to Sherman, but in avoiding the railroad, he had ridden east. That put him northeast of Sherman and a good distance for horseback riding from Hen-

rietta, his immediate destination. He had quite a ride ahead
of him, but that was all right, too. Let the Jessups and that
damned Colfax wonder what had become of him. Let them
stew awhile for a change. He mounted up and headed the
horse west. He figured that he had about a hundred miles to
ride. He'd take it easy. Give himself at least three days for
the trip. Tubby had given him a good supply of trail food.
He'd relax, work the stiffness out of his muscles, and plan.

Luton figured right. No one knew where he had gone. At
least no one found him anywhere between Sherman and Henrietta. By the time he reached Henrietta, he felt rested, re-
freshed, and ready to tie into the Jessups. He wasn't so sure
about Colfax. It wasn't that he was afraid of Colfax. He had
no reason to fight Colfax—no desire to kill him. At the same
time, he didn't want Colfax getting in his way, and he certainly didn't want Colfax killing him before he got his job
done. He realized that that was a very real possibility. He
would have to be extremely cautious.

The trip had taken two and a half days, and when he
reached Henrietta it was daylight. He decided that he didn't
want to chance being seen. Not just yet. So he made a cold
camp where the Little Wichita River ran close by the town.
Before the night was black, he longed for a fire. He was
chilly, even wrapped snugly in his blankets. He waited for
the darkness to set in well, then he saddled up his horse once
more and headed toward the town. He decided to ease in on
a back street and poke around a bit. With any luck, he might
find the hotel without having to ask for information. He hoped
so. That would call less attention to him. He found nothing
with Harold Decker's name on it, but there was only one
reputable looking hotel in the town which was beginning to
take on the general characteristics of a terminus town. He
decided to try the Cross Timbers Hotel.

Inside the lobby he found only the man behind the counter.
It was late, and that was what he had hoped for. He walked
over to the desk, and the man came to meet him.

"Can I help you, sir?"

"You wouldn't be Mr. Decker by any chance?" said Luton.

"Yes, I am."

"Well, Mr. Decker, I'm Sarge Luton. I wonder if you could tell me if Mrs. Fisher and her son arrived safely on the train."

"Mr. Luton," said Decker, offering a hand for Luton to shake, "I'm real pleased to meet you. Emily told me what a help you were to her on the trip. Yes, she's here, and she's just fine. Her and little Matt. They're both just fine. You know, this is the first time I've ever seen that boy."

"He's a fine boy, Mr. Decker."

"Mr. Luton, I owe you for what you've done for them. Anything I can do for you, just ask. Can I get you a room?"

"Well," said Luton, "you might be able to give me a little information. I'm looking for Will Milam. He's an old friend of mine. I understand that he's lost his ranch, so I don't know where to look for him."

"That's easy, Mr. Luton," said Decker.

"I'd be more comfortable if you'd call me 'Sarge.' "

"Okay, Sarge. Will's got a room right here. Right upstairs. He's been here since he lost the ranch."

"Mr. Decker, I believe that I'll take you up on that offer of a room."

"One condition."

"What's that?"

"Call me 'Hal.' "

For the first time since he had left Riddle, Luton slept on a bed. And in spite of the many things tormenting his mind that might under other circumstances have kept him awake long into the night, he slept well, and when he awoke the following morning feeling fresh and better rested than he had felt in days, he remembered no fitful dreams from the night before.

* * *

Will Milam sat at a table in the dining room of the Cross
Timbers. He was eating the same breakfast he always ordered, four fried eggs, fried potatoes, a rasher of bacon,
biscuits, and gravy. He was slurping his coffee between bites
when a stranger walked up to the table and pulled out a chair.
He looked up quickly, his heavy dark brows coming together
between his eyes in a scowl.

"There's other tables," he said.

"I like this one."

Milam studied the stranger's face, his own expression turning quizzical. The stranger sat down.

"You don't know me, Will?"

"Bluff Luton?" said Milam, his voice a harsh whisper.
"Bluff, is that you?"

"It's me," said Luton, "but let's keep it as quiet as we
can for a while yet."

"Bluff Luton. Goddamn. You're damned right it's been
that long. Have you et?"

"No, and I could sure stand a good meal."

Will Milam half stood up from his seat and waved frantically at a waiter across the room.

"Hey. Hey, Silas," he said. "Come take this man's order."

Oliver Colfax strode into the ranch house that had once
been the home of Will Milam. The Jessup brothers were
lounging in the living room, Toad sprawled out on the couch
and Jasper sitting in a large easy chair on his spine. Each had
a bottle of whiskey. Toad was chewing tobacco and spitting
on the floor. Jasper smoked a large, foul-smelling cigar. A
mongrel hound slept in the center of the floor. When Colfax
appeared, Toad sat up quickly.

"You see him?" he said.

"Nope," said Colfax. "He's not been seen yet in these
parts."

"Damn it," said Toad. "Why the hell didn't you kill him
when you had him on the train? Now we got to worry about

him sneaking up on us down here. I wanted him dead before he ever got back to Texas."

"What the hell we paying you for anyway?" said Jasper, still lounging on his spine.

Toad spat juice onto the floor and stepped toward his brother.

"Be careful, Jasper," he said. "We ain't paid him nothing. We pay when he delivers. Remember?"

"That may be never."

"Your brother gave you some good advice," said Colfax. "Be careful what you say. Especially to me."

"I don't think he's anybody to worry about, Toad," Jasper sneered. "Anybody that let the chances he had go by, he's probably lost his nerve."

Colfax turned to walk out of the house, but as he came alongside the chair in which Jasper sat, he grabbed it by the back and turned it over. Jasper's head banged against the floor and his legs flew up over his head. Before he could react, he saw Colfax standing over him, the big Colt aimed between his eyes.

"I usually don't kill a man except for pay," said Colfax, "but if you don't watch your mouth, I might be happy to make an exception out of you."

He replaced the Colt in his high holster and walked to the door. He paused, turned to face the brothers once more.

"I'll make my move when I'm ready. Not before. I'll let you know when it's done."

Will Milam had purchased a bottle of medium-priced brandy and taken it, along with Bluff Luton, upstairs in the Cross Timbers to his room. He offered Luton a chair and he sat on the bed. They passed the bottle back and forth as they talked.

"I know why you're here," said Milam. "The word's all over. The Jessups sent you a phony message. That I sent word for you that they was here. That right?"

"That's right," said Luton. "I believed it at first, but I

figured out that you hadn't sent the message. I figured that
they did it themselves, knowing that I'd come after them.
Then they set up their ambushes for me along the way. What
I don't know is how they knew where to send for me, and
why, after all these years, they chose to go after me now.''

"That's easy. There was a newspaper story circulated
around here not long ago. Said something about you cleaning
up that town in Iowa. Course I didn't read it myself. You
know I can't read. But I was told about it. Alf told me. You
recall Alf?''

"No. I don't know any Alf.''

"Yeah, you do. Maybe you don't know his name or you
forgot it, but you know him. He's the man ran that trading
post in Wichita Falls. Remember?''

"Oh, yeah,'' said Luton. "I know him. I don't think I
ever heard his name.''

"It's Alf.''

"So he told you about the story?''

"Yeah. And folks was talking about you. I guess the Jessups heard, and I guess they figured that if they found out
where you was at, you might be able to find out where they
was. They know you want them, so they decided to try to
get you first.''

Milam took a long swig from the bottle and handed it to
Luton.

"All right,'' said Luton, "so I'm here to get the Jessups,
and the Jessups are gunning for me. There's something else
I don't know.''

"What's that?''

"How the hell did the Jessups get your ranch away from
you?''

Milam took back the bottle and drew a long draft on it
again. He wiped his mouth with his sleeve and let out a long
and tired sigh. Then he stood up, handed the bottle back to
Luton, and began pacing the floor.

"It's a long story, Bluff,'' he said.

"I got all day.''

"It happened after the war. The Yankees sent those damn carpetbaggers down here to run things. You know."

"Yeah. You know, I fought with the Yankees."

"Oh, hell, Bluff, I know that, but you stayed up there after the war. You didn't come back here to lord it over your old friends. I always respected you for that. You ain't no damned scallywag."

"But the Jessups?"

"Scallywags. The worst kind. I don't know how they got in with them carpetbaggers, but they did somehow. They got in real good with them."

"So how did they get your ranch?"

"Hell, I'm coming to that. You know, I got that place with old land certificates. They was still good, and back then we didn't have no real organized county government. Alf, he kept all the county records. My deal wasn't never registered with the state. I guess you knowed I never was too bright. The Jessups went to the county carpetbag government with a paper they said I'd signed selling them my property. Had witnesses, they said. You know I can't write. It had a X on it."

"And they gave them your ranch on that basis?"

"They're still sitting on it."

"What's your local government like these days?"

"Ain't nothing much left of it. The Jessups have got a gang of gunfighters they call range detectives. They ain't legal."

"That's all?"

"Hell, Bluff, there still ain't much civilization in Wichita County. It ain't like over here in Clay County, or even Montague County. The Jessups has got the power."

"Just how much power do they have, Will? How many gunslingers?"

"Well, let me see now. They've got almost all of my old boys, but they ain't gunfighters, they're cowboys. All but Curly Wade. He was my foreman. He quit when they evicted me off the place. I told him not to. Told him a job is a job, but he wouldn't listen. Ain't found a steady job since."

"So how many of these 'range detectives' have they got?"

"I think there's five of them right now. Let's see. There's Billy Bob Handley, Jordan Bradley, Woody Barnett, Rat Face—Rat Face what's his name?—Hanks. That's it. Rat Face Hanks, and then there's Simpson. I don't know his other name. Simpson."

"That's five," said Luton.

"Yeah. Five. That's what I said, ain't it? Five."

Luton looked at his old friend. Milam looked old. True, it had been a number of years, and Luton was older, too, but Milam looked old, tired, beat, and a little embarrassed. Luton's hatred for the Jessups intensified, seeing what they had done to Will Milam. Maybe he could get them and get back Milam's ranch for him at the same time. Maybe.

"Will," he said, "sit down and listen to me. Listen good. Did the Jessups register their claim to your place with the state?"

"Well, now, let me see. I don't believe so, Bluff. Far as I know, all they done was just to file the papers over at Alf's place and run me off. I don't believe they ever went to the state."

Now it was Luton's turn to rise and pace the floor. He scratched his head. Things seemed pretty unorganized in Wichita County. But that's good, he thought. That's real good.

"Will," he said, "what do you reckon would happen if somebody was to kill the Jessups and either kill or run off those so-called detectives of theirs and get that paper back from Alf and tear it up? What do you suppose would happen then?"

"Why, I don't reckon anybody outside of the county would ever know the difference, and nobody in it would give a damn. I reckon I'd have my place back."

"You want your place back bad enough to fight for it?"

"You damn right."

Milam was up on his feet again, and his tired features were showing signs of renewed life.

"You goddamn right," he said again. "Tell me what to do."

"Is there anyone else we can count on around here for some help?"

"Yeah," said Milam. "Curly. My old foreman. Curly'll help us. I know he will."

"That's three against seven," said Luton. "Maybe eight."

"Who's eight?"

"A hired killer named Colfax. I left him up in the Indian Territory with a split skull. He'll be after me."

"Three against eight," said Milam.

"I've seen worse odds, Will. Right now we got to do some serious planning. I want you to ride out with me and show me the lay of the land. I want to see your ranch. See where they hang out."

Milam reached in a dresser drawer and pulled out a gun belt holding a Remington Frontier .44. He strapped it around his waist. It was just a little snug.

"Let's go," he said. "A little while back in the saddle and this'll fit just fine again."

Chapter Fourteen

"How much farther till we get to your range?" said Luton.

"Hell," said Milam, "we're on it now. Have been for a while. It's still a ways to the ranch house. You can't tell coming in from this direction. Used to couldn't tell from any direction, but the damned Jessup brothers has got the boys to fencing the east and west boundaries. They just ain't got around to this southern one yet. I don't hold with bob wire myself, but I guess it's coming no matter how I feel."

"This land is flat as a griddle cake," said Luton. "Does it stay like this clean up to the house?"

"Yep."

"What about coming at it from the north? How far is the river away from the house?"

"Too damn far to give us any cover sneaking up, if that's what you're getting at. Ain't no way to sneak up on that house."

That was exactly what Luton had been thinking about. He had figured that the lay of the land would be flat and barren, but he had hoped for a surprise, a little knoll or something. But the open landscape was exactly the reason they had started this ride at midnight, planning to sight the house about dawn. Luton wanted to get a good look at the place in order to better

plan his strategy. Riding back to town would be no problem.
He wasn't planning any action this morning, although he had
to consider the possibility that he would be seen. If so, his
whereabouts would no longer be a secret. He would lose that
advantage. *But*, he thought, *it has to come sooner or later.
And right now, I'm thinking, the sooner the better.*

"Up ahead," said Milam.

Luton reined in his mount alongside Milam, who was
pointing ahead through the hazy light of the breaking day,
and he made out the gray shape of the ranch house. There
were other shapes around it.

"Let's ease on up," he said. "I want a better look."

They rode up closer, and as they did, the sky lightened a
bit more. Luton halted his mount again.

"Hold it, Will," he said. "This is close enough for now."

In spite of what Luton had said earlier about the flatness
of the ground, he found himself on a slight rise. Down at the
bottom of the slope, a road ran almost east and west, cutting
across the scene that lay before him. Off to his left, a second
road ran northeast, making an acute angle with the first.
Bordering the northeast road on the far side was a small
corral with some interior cross-fencing adjacent to a low-
roofed stable. At the north end of the fence a windmill stood
stark against the reddening sky. Sweeping his gaze to the
east, or to his own right, Luton found beyond the windmill
a small stack of hay bales, the ranch house, which was a
medium-sized frame structure of only one floor, and then a
small grove of trees. Beyond was more of the near-level prairie.

"Nope," he said, "there'll be no taking them by surprise."

"Then what'll we do?" said Milam.

"When the time comes," said Luton, "we'll just have to
challenge them dead on."

Will Milam pulled out his Frontier .44.

"Then, by God," he said, "there's no time like the present."

"Hold it, Will. There's only the two of us."

"One more won't make that much difference."

"One more might make a hell of a lot of difference. Put that damn gun away and listen to me. We don't even know who's down there right now. We've seen what I wanted to see for now. Let's ride back to town and do some planning."

Luton wanted as much help as he could get. This whole operation had turned out to be much more than he had bargained for. He had started his trip to Texas believing that he would face the Jessups alone. It was because of Bud, and it was between Luton and Bud's killers—or so Luton had thought. That had been before he had known of the Jessups' hired killers, their "range detectives," Colfax, and the loss of Will Milam's ranch to the Jessups. There was much more to consider now than there had been at the beginning of this trek. Now he wanted help. If Will and Curly were all he could get, then they would have to do. And if Curly was willing, as Milam had said he would be, then Luton for sure wasn't going to attack the ranch without him. Three could be significantly better than two.

He also wanted to find out as much as he could about the habits of the Jessups and their gang of five. Were they all at the ranch house together at regular times? Did the five stay somewhere else? Were there regular trips to town? If so, who made them and when? There might be ways to approach this problem without mounting a full-scale attack on the fortress, but even if the only approach turned out to be that full-scale attack, Luton wanted all of the enemy to be holed up in the fortress at one time. No sense in dragging this business out any longer than necessary, he thought.

He wondered where Colfax was. He knew that he hadn't killed the man—just inconvenienced him some. Colfax would be back on his trail—he knew that, too. He might even be on the ranch or in Henrietta already. He could be watching Luton's every move. Luton had had the sense before, during the train ride, that when he was totally unaware of Colfax's

presence, the killer was keeping an eye on him from some
hiding place.

And finally, before the showdown, there were two more
things that Luton wanted to do. He wanted to go by the
trading post at Wichita Falls and talk to Alf to find out for
sure what would happen to the deed to Milam's ranch if he
was successful. Was it certain that the Jessups had not registered their claim with the state? If they had, then it would
be useless to try to get the ranch back for Milam. If they
hadn't, then was Will correct in assuming that all they would
have to do would be to throw away the fraudulent paper the
Jessups had produced? Luton felt that it was necessary to
find out the truth about this matter. If it was not going to be
possible to get the ranch back for Will, then there was no
reason to risk the lives of Will and Curly. It would be back
to the simpler and more straightforward plot of Luton's revenge for his murdered brother. The other thing he wanted
to do before making a move on the Jessups, just in case it
turned out wrong, was to visit once more with Emily Fisher.
He had promised her that he would see her in Texas, and so
far he had not kept that promise.

Back at the Cross Timbers, Luton suggested that Milam
look up Curly and bring him around for a meeting that night.
Then he went to the desk to see Hal Decker.

"Hal," he said, "is Emily around?"

"She's up in her room, Sarge."

"Would it be all right if I was to look in on her? Just for
a few minutes. I promised her before I left the train up in
Indian Territory that I would do that, and I may not get another chance."

"Sure, Sarge. Go right on up and knock. I think the boy's
out playing, but she's up there."

Luton stood with his hat in his hands, feeling a little awkward as Emily opened the door. He really had no idea what
he was going to say to her.

"Hello, Sarge," she said. "I knew that you were in town. Won't you come in?"

"Do you think that it would look right?"

"We'll leave the door open. Come on in."

Luton stepped heavily into the room, keeping his eyes on the floor.

"Are you all right?" he said.

"Just fine. Thank you."

"And the boy?"

"Fine. He's already made some new friends. They're out playing right now."

"I wanted to come by and see you, because, well, because I said that I would. To make sure that everything was all right with you and Matt. But I also wanted to come by to tell you good-bye. I've got a job to do, and when it's done, I'll be leaving Texas."

"You're going to kill some men, aren't you?"

Luton looked up at Emily, a little surprised.

"I'm not sequestered in here," she said. "I've heard the talk."

"They killed my brother. It was a long time ago, but I never knew where they were until now."

"And that Mr. Colfax?"

"He's working for them."

"He's not the only one, from what I've heard," said Emily.

"No, he's not."

"You could be killed."

"Yes. I suppose so."

"I wish you didn't have to do it."

Luton shuffled his feet and played with the brim of his hat. Ordinarily he would have enjoyed the company of this woman very much, but just now he was getting more and more restless, more nervous, anxious for the conversation to end. He had kept his promise. He had paid her a visit in Texas, and she was all right.

"Well," he said, "are you sure that you're safe here from . . ."

He didn't finish the question, but she knew the rest of it.

"I don't think George will come down here after us," she said, "or send anyone else. Not after what happened to Ryan. Thank you."

But Luton read in her expression a hint of uncertainty, a little fear.

"I have to go now, Emily," he said, and he turned and walked to the door, but before going on through, he turned back to face her once more. "If I come out of this scrape alive," he said, "I'll make sure of it. I promise you that."

He turned again quickly and walked through the door and on down the hallway, not giving her a chance to reply, and he wondered just how the hell he intended to keep that rash promise.

It was well past dark when Luton heard a knock on his door in the Cross Timbers. He took up his Starr in his right hand and moved to the door.

"Who is it?" he said.

"It's Will. Open up."

Luton lowered the pistol and opened the door. Will Milam stepped quickly into the room, followed by a young cowboy.

"This here's Curly," he said. Then he gestured toward Luton and added, "Bluff Luton."

"Howdy, Bluff," said Curly. "I understand we're going to take Will's ranch back for him."

"We're going to talk about the possibilities," said Luton. "Sit down."

Curly turned a straight chair around and stepped over it like he was climbing into a saddle, then laid his forearms across the back.

"All right," he said. "Let's talk."

"Can you handle those irons you're wearing?" said Luton.

"I can shoot."

"He's a hell of a scrapper," said Milam.

"This is going to take more than scrapping," said Luton. "We're going up against some professional killers."

Curly bristled, and Luton could tell that the man felt insulted.

"You don't have to worry about me," said Curly. "I can handle myself. Matter of fact, I'm just a little worried about you old guys."

"I think we'll hold up," said Luton, but he wondered about the truth of what he had just said. Curly will do, he thought. He got three glasses from a cupboard and handed one each to Milam and Curly, then picked up a bottle of rye whiskey and poured them each a drink. He sat down on the edge of the bed. Milam was leaning against the wall when he wasn't pacing the floor. *Curly will do. I'm not so sure about Will. Or me.*

"You got a plan?" said Curly.

"That's what we're here for," said Luton. "We have to know as much as we can find out about the habits of the Jessups and their five hired guns. Where do they all stay? Are they ever all in the ranch house at once? Do they make regular trips to town? Anything like that we can find out."

"I can find out that stuff," said Curly. "Some of the boys out there are still loyal to me and to Mr. Milam. I can trust them, and they'll tell me anything I want to know."

"Can you get that information tomorrow?"

"I think so."

"Well," said Luton, "do your best. Me and Will are going to take a little trip over to Wichita Falls while you're doing that. Let's get together right here again tomorrow night. Same time."

"What the hell are we going to Wichita Falls for?" said Milam.

Luton emptied his glass and looked at Milam.

"We're going to pay a visit to Alf," he said. "I'll knock on your door about five."

* * *

In a line shack out on the disputed rangeland, Oliver Colfax rolled a cigarette, leaned back to stretch out on a thin
cot, and put his left hand behind his head. He winced as he
felt the still-sore spot where Sarge Luton had bashed him
from behind. *His time will come,* he thought. *He wants two
men. Maybe he has good reason to want them dead, but in
order to get what he wants, he'll have to go through five
more. Will he kill five men he doesn't even know just to get
at two he wants? If so, I've got him right where I want him.*

> Why, let the stricken deer go weep,
> The hart ungalled play;
> For some must watch, while some must sleep:
> So runs the world away.

He thought of Hamlet and how badly the poor man had
wanted to kill his stepfather, and he thought of his own childhood and the stepfather he had wanted so badly to kill. He
remembered with love and loathing the mother who had so
quickly, to his young mind, replaced a father killed in a
southern Illinois feud between two families, no one member
of which could remember how or why the feud had begun.
It was no mystery to Colfax why he found *Hamlet,* among
the works of the Bard, so particularly appealing. But enough
of *Hamlet* and enough of foolish, sentimental childhood
memories, he thought. He tossed the butt of his cigarette
onto the dirt floor of the shack, stood up, and moved to the
small table and chair across the room, where he sat down to
clean and oil his Colt. *Keep your mind on business, Cole,* he
told himself. *The time is nigh. Killing time is almost here.*

> Let Hercules himself do what he may,
> The cat will mew and dog will have his day.

Luton was even better than his word. It was not yet five
o'clock the following morning when he knocked at the door
of Will Milam's room in the Cross Timbers. Will answered

the door soon enough, even though he was not quite ready to go. But very soon the two men were mounted up and riding toward the trading post at Wichita Falls.

"I still don't know what the hell we're doing this for," said Milam.

"Will, we don't know whether or not the Jessups have registered their claim with the state. If they did, then there's no sense you getting involved in this thing. You might get killed, and all for nothing. We've got to go see Alf to find out just exactly what is the status of your land. You understand what I'm telling you?"

"Yeah, I think so."

"And don't be so all-fired impatient about charging off to kill someone. It ain't a matter to be taken lightly, and even if that don't soak in your thick skull, you ought to understand that we need to do some careful planning before we stick our necks out. The odds are already in their favor. We want to do everything we can to try to even out those odds."

"Hell," said Milam, "you're right. I know. It's just that I had given up a long time ago, and then you come in after them two and got my hopes up again. Don't worry. I'm all right. And you're calling the shots."

Although the setting had changed somewhat over the years—there were a few more scattered buildings and more signs of life than Luton recalled from long ago—he recognized the old trading post at once, and the memories flooded back. He fought them off by concentrating on present problems. They tied their horses at the hitching rail just outside and walked into the trading post. Alf looked a little older, but otherwise pretty much the same. Luton thought that he'd have recognized the man anywhere, then realized that he was deluding himself about the effect of the years. Walking into the trading post, he knew who to expect. Probably if he had run into Alf somewhere else, say St. Jo, he wouldn't have known him from Useless Grant.

"Will Milam, what the hell brings you around these parts?" said Alf.

"I brought somebody to see you," said Milam, "from way back."

Alf squinted at Luton.

"Yeah?"

"This here's Bluff Luton, Alf," said Milam. "Remember?"

"By God. Yes, by God. What are you doing back here?"

Alf took Luton by the hand and pumped vigorously.

"We need some information," said Luton. "I understand you keep the county records here. That right?"

"That's right."

"What can you tell us about Will's ranch?"

"You mean the Jessup place," said Alf.

"Call it what you like," said Luton. "What's its legal status?"

"I've got a document filed that says that Will sold the place to the Jessup brothers. It was witnessed by three men, signed by both Jessups and by Will with his mark."

"That's a goddamned lie," said Milam.

"Just stay calm, Will," said Luton. "I think you know that paper's a fraud as much as we do, Alf. Is it the only claim the Jessups have to the place?"

"Well, they're sitting on it. Possession counts for something, don't it?"

"Yeah, it does," said Luton, "and we're considering a repossession. Have they filed their claim with the state?"

"Naw. Never have."

"Are you sure? They might have done it without telling you about it."

"Couldn't have," said Alf. "They'd have had to taken this paper with them. It's been right here in my safe the whole time."

"That's good," said Luton. "That's good. One more question."

"Yeah. Sure."

"What would your position on this whole matter of legal ownership be if me and Will here was to run them Jessups and their gun hands off the place? If it was Will sitting back there where he belongs?"

Alf shifted his eyes back and forth nervously. There was no one else in the trading post, no one to overhear anything that was being said, yet he kept his voice low when he responded to Luton's final query.

"Just between you and me and Will," he said, "I never did like them two. I didn't like it when they come back here after the war. I'd been hoping that you had caught up with them and done them in. If they was really taken care of, I mean really out of the way for good, that there sale paper could just kind of disappear. You know what I mean?"

"I don't believe I know you," said Luton.

"Mister, you're gonna know me real good before I leave," ...

Chapter Fifteen

Luton and Milam rode slowly into Henrietta, heading toward the Cross Timbers. It was about time for their meeting with Curly, the trip to Wichita Falls and back having taken the whole day.

"Will Curly wait?" Luton asked.

"He'll wait," said Milam. "Matter of fact, I see his horse down yonder."

Luton felt good about the visit to Alf. The news had been what he had hoped he would hear. It was possible to get the ranch back for Will Milam—possible if not easy. The day had been well spent, but now Luton had the biggest problem of all to solve. He would have to talk to Will and Curly about it in a short while. They rode into the stable just down the street from the Cross Timbers and put the horses away for the night, then walked on down to the hotel. Milam had just put his hand on the doorknob when they heard the voice from out in the street.

"Luton."

Luton turned to look. Across the street and down a couple of doors, two men stood facing him. They wore long-tailed, dark coats, the tails shoved back to reveal the six-guns hanging at their hips.

"I don't believe I know you," said Luton.

Milam eased up beside Luton and whispered to him in a harsh voice.

"Jessups' range detectives," he said.

"I'm Billy Bob Handley," said the man across the street, "and this here's Woody Barnett."

"What business do you have with me?" said Luton.

"We have reason to believe that you came here to murder our employers," said Billy Bob.

Luton spoke softly to Will Milam.

"Will," he said, "get inside."

"The hell I will."

"Will, we don't want to tip our hand just yet. Get inside."

Milam pulled open the door and stepped into the Cross Timbers. Luton stepped down into the street and took a couple of steps toward Billy Bob and Woody.

"Just who is it that you gentlemen work for?" he asked.

"The Jessup Ranch."

"I never heard of the Jessup Ranch," said Luton. "Is that around here somewhere?"

"Used to belong to Will Milam," said Woody.

"Shut up, Woody," said Billy Bob. "He knows what the hell it is. Let's get on with it, Luton."

"I don't know what you're talking about," said Luton. "You never did tell me what business you have with me."

"We're here to stop you from killing the Jessups."

Luton thought carefully. Killing these two here and now would not do any good. It would simply put the others on guard, maybe even provoke them into attacking. On the other hand, they were obviously onto him already, but they probably didn't know anything about his being joined by Milam and Curly. For all they knew, it was just him coming to get the Jessups. They would have no way of knowing about the plans to restore the ranch to Will Milam.

"You're not stopping me from anything but going upstairs to my room to try to get a good night's sleep," he said. "Do I look like I'm trying to kill someone?"

"You're a yellow-bellied Yankee," said Woody.

"Are you two trying to provoke me into a fight? Is that what you're up to?"

Luton spoke loudly for the benefit of the few onlookers who were still out on the street late at night. He noticed that Woody was getting edgy. Billy Bob was cool. He decided that Woody would probably be the first one to make a move, but that if he was forced to fight here and now, he would go for Billy Bob first.

"I'll tell you the truth, boys," he said. "I did come here to settle an old score with the Jessup brothers. It's something personal from a long time ago. I've got no reason to fight with you. I have no desire to kill you. I don't even know you. I'd appreciate it if you would just stay out of this and let me settle things with the Jessups. There's two of them and just one of me anyhow. Fair enough?

"Now I'm going to turn around and go inside the hotel. I trust you won't shoot me in the back in front of witnesses."

Luton turned his back and took a few steps toward the sidewalk, just as Woody went for his gun. The front door of the Cross Timbers flew open and Will Milam stepped out onto the sidewalk with his Remington held out at arm's length.

"Look out, Bluff," he shouted, and he pulled the trigger.

Luton threw himself forward into the dirt and rolled, fumbling for his Starr, as Milam stepped to one side and Curly came out of the door behind him. Across the street Woody leaned back against the wall behind him, clutching a broken and bloody shoulder. Billy Bob drew his pistol, but he hesitated. His main target was rolling in the dirt, but there were two new threats across the street from him. That moment's hesitation cost him his life. Curly fired two shots into his chest, and Billy Bob jerked, then pitched forward into the street. Woody bent over in a panic and picked up his fallen handgun in his left hand. He screamed and fired two wild shots across the street. Will Milam took careful aim and dropped him with one shot.

Luton stood up in the sudden silence. He looked at the two bodies and reholstered his Starr, then dusted himself off and walked over to where Milam and Curly stood. The first battle was over and won and Luton had not fired a shot.

"Well," he said, "there's no turning back now. We're all into it all the way."

"There wasn't never going to be no turning back," said Curly.

"That narrows the odds a mite," said Milam. "Two down. Six to go."

There was a sudden pounding of hooves, and a horse and rider appeared out of the darkness from between two buildings, turned, and headed out of town.

"Rat Face," said Milam, and he pointed his Remington. Luton took hold of Milam's wrist.

"Let it go, Will," he said. "You've killed enough tonight. You'd never hit him anyway."

"Damn," said Milam.

"Well," said Curly, "a surprise attack is out of the question now."

"Yeah," said Luton. "Let's go inside and talk."

Across the street in the shadows of a law office closed tight for the night, Oliver Colfax struck a match on the side of the building to light his cigarette. *That son of a bitch,* he thought. *He's still a jump ahead of me.*

"What did you find out?" said Luton.

"It don't make no difference now," said Curly. "After Rat Face tells the Jessups what we done tonight, they'll most likely change all their habits."

"Tell us anyway."

"Well, tomorrow's Friday, and it's payday. Ordinarily on a payday, the punchers all head into town soon as they draw their pay. All except the ones who has to work, and that ain't many. That leaves the Jessups at the ranch house without a crew around them, so they keep their detectives in the house with them for protection."

"So if we hadn't run into these three tonight," Luton said, "we'd most likely have been able to catch them all together tomorrow night? Right?"

"Right."

"What about Colfax?"

"Nobody knows nothing about that one," said Curly. "He's been seen at the ranch a couple of times, but he don't seem to have no regular habits. No one knows where he stays or nothing."

"That sounds like him," said Luton. "He's the uncertainty in the whole thing. We can't plan for him. We'll just have to be ready for him whenever he shows himself."

"What do you suppose they'll do now, Curly?" said Milam.

"I don't know."

Luton paced across the floor. He rubbed his shoulder where he had banged it on the street dodging the bullets of Woody and Billy Bob, and he thought again of how old he was getting and how soft his job in Iowa had made him. He turned back to face Milam and Curly.

"I think we have to figure that they'll do just what they usually do. When they find out that two of their men have been killed, that'll be all the more reason for them to hole up in the ranch house and keep their bodyguards close. The only thing they might do different, they might keep the cowboys around for numbers."

"They might," said Curly, "but if they do, I can take care of that."

"Okay," said Luton. "Then that will leave the three of us to deal with five of them fortified inside the house, and watching over our shoulders at all times for the appearance of Colfax."

The three men sat quietly and looked at one another for a long moment. Colfax's expression came to Luton's mind. It's killing time. The words irritated him. He stood up.

"Tomorrow night," he said.

* * *

"I heard the shots and I looked out and there was Woody and Billy Bob both laying dead in the street," Rat Face said. "I rode hard out of there."

"Luton done it?" said Toad Jessup.

"I didn't see it," said Rat Face. "Like I said, I heard the shots, then I looked out and they was already dead. Luton was there, but he wasn't alone."

"So who was with him?" said Jasper. "Do we got to drag every word out of you?"

"Will Milam was there, and so was Curly."

"Damn."

Toad Jessup sprang up from his chair and paced nervously across the room.

"Damn," he said again. "That old bastard Milam and that damn Curly. Three of them now. Three. Where the hell is Colfax?"

"Rat Face," said Jasper, "you go out and find Colfax. He's got to kill them."

"Wait a minute, goddamn it," said Toad. "We've only just got three men left to guard us here. If he goes out looking for Colfax, what happens if they show up here while he's gone? You think about that? We need everyone here in case they show up. They're going to show up. They're coming to kill us. You know that?"

"Well, what do we do?" said Jasper. "Just sit here and wait for them?"

"Yeah," said Toad. "Yeah. That's exactly what we'll do. Simpson and Jordan are out front on the porch. Rat Face will be out back. You and me will be inside. We'll wait. Hell, our men will be able to pick them off easy if they come riding out here. Ain't no way they can sneak up on us. Is there?"

"No. No, there ain't. We'll wait. Rat Face, get on out back and watch. Where the hell is that damned Colfax?"

It was a dark night, but Curly knew where he was going. He rode up near enough the line shack so that he knew his voice could be heard.

"Hello," he shouted. "The cabin."

He couldn't see it, but he could hear the door creak slightly open. He knew that there would be a gun poking out through the crack. He listened for the voice.

"Who's out there?" it said.

"It's Curly Wade."

"Curly? What you doing here, boy?"

"Is that you, Joe?"

"Yeah, come on in."

Curly nudged his horse on up to the cabin and dismounted. He slapped a hitch around the short rail by the front door and went inside. A dim light from a coal oil lantern gave the small room a dingy illumination. There were two small cots in the room and two straight chairs beside a small table. An iron potbellied stove stood in one corner, and there was just enough chill in the night air for Joe to have built up a small fire.

"You got coffee on?" asked Curly.

He could see and smell the coffee, so the question was rhetorical, and it had the desired effect.

"Sure," said Joe. "You want a cup?"

"You damn rights."

Joe poured two cups and handed one to Curly. The cowboys sat down across from each other at the small table.

"Damn, Curly," said Joe, "I ain't seen you in a while. How you been, boy?"

"Doing all right, I guess. Tomorrow payday?"

"You know it is. You need a loan?"

"Naw," said Curly, "that ain't what I come out here for."

He took a long slurp of the hot coffee. Joe reached into his shirt pocket and withdrew the makings.

"Smoke?" he said.

"Yeah."

Curly accepted the makings from Joe and rolled himself a cigarette, handing the tiny pouch and the papers back to Joe. Joe rolled one for himself, repocketed the makings, and produced a match. He scratched the match on the table, lit Curly's cigarette and then his own.

"So," he said, "what is it then? You didn't ride all the way out here in the middle of the night just only to pay me a visit."

"Got a big favor to ask, Joe," said Curly as he blew out a lungful of smoke.

"All you got to do is just ask."

"Come time to collect your pay tomorrow, I want you and the rest of the boys to just ride into town. Don't go by the house to get your pay. Don't show yourselves over there at all. Just ride off the ranch."

"That's asking a lot, Curly. We all been working a month waiting for payday. You got a reason?"

"I know it's asking a lot. I said it was a big favor, didn't I? How you like punching cows for the Jessups?"

"Not worth a damn," said Joe. "They don't neither one of them know a cow from a bull. And they're nasty tempered as anyone I ever seen. Me and the other boys all would have quit when you did, Curly. You know that. You told us not to do it. Told us to hang on to our jobs. You remember that."

"I know," said Curly. He took a long drag on his cigarette, then pitched it toward the stove. It landed on the dirt floor a little short of its mark. "Something's come up, Joe. Me and Mr. Milam, we're coming out here tomorrow to take this place back."

"Just the two of you?"

"One other man."

Joe stood up and walked to the stove for the coffeepot. He carried it to the table and refilled the cups, then put it back on the stove top.

"Curly," he said, "there's the two Jessups, and then there's them five gunfighters they call detectives. Maybe more. I hear they've been hiring gunmen to protect them from somebody."

"There may be one gunfighter around. We don't know.

As far as them detectives are concerned, there's only three of them now.''

"You're serious about this thing."

"Never more serious in my life. After what happened to their detectives, we figured that when you boys showed up for your pay, the Jessups might try to keep you around the house. Try to make you help fight us off.''

"I'll fix it with all the boys," said Joe. "There won't be none of us there when you show up.''

Bluff Luton was on his back. He could feel his own blood seeping and soaking his shirt. He couldn't feel any pain, but he was weak, so weak he couldn't move. Bud came toward him and knelt to hold up his head. He knew it was Bud, even though he was seeing through a haze. It wasn't a real haze. He knew that. It was a haze of his own, produced by his hurt and his weakness. Even through the haze, he could read the fear and confusion on the young face that leaned over him— could see the panic setting in. Then he saw the two figures loom up from somewhere off in the fog. They moved closer, got bigger, became clearer, and he recognized them. The Jessups. The one called Toad was holding a shotgun, and he leveled it at Bud's back. Bud heard their approach and stood, turning to face them. The finger on the trigger tightened, and Luton's vision of the world was suddenly focused entirely on the trigger and the trigger guard and the tightening finger, a dirty finger. Then the blast, a loud deafening roar, and there was no longer any picture, no longer anything to see. He had no vision. There was only the vast blackness and the resounding echo of the explosion in his head.

Luton's eyes popped open wide, and he sat up quickly and stiffly in bed. He stared ahead into the darkness of the room, not knowing for a long instant just where he was. He was sweating. He could feel the droplets rolling down the side of his head from his temples. He took deep breaths, and he slowly remembered that he was sleeping in a room in the Cross Timbers Hotel in Henrietta, Texas, and that he was going to rise soon to dress and arm himself and ride out to deliberately kill two men. He knew, also, that in order to accomplish this task, he might well have to kill others. And he knew that in trying to do this deed, it could easily be he who would die on the dusty plain of north Texas.

He crawled out of the bed and walked to the stand which held the washbasin. He dipped his hands into the stale water and splashed some into his face. Then he picked up the dirty towel and wiped away the mingled stale wash water and salty sweat. He tossed the towel aside and moved to the window to stare out into the night.

"Either way," he said, "that was the last dream."

Chapter Sixteen

Joe and the other cowboys from the ranch rode together into Wichita Falls to hang around the trading post. It was a place to kind of hide out from the action, a place to wait and see. It was also a place where the hot and dry cowboys could get a few drinks. Alf was always good for a little credit. He was also good for conversation, and he might even know a little more about what was going on with Will Milam and Curly Wade. At the trading post, Joe was the first of the cowboys to burst through the door.

"Hello, Joe," said Alf. Then, seeing the other punchers crowd into the room, he added, "Damn. What brings all you boys in here?"

"We need some drinks," said Joe. "On the tab, if you please. We had to miss our payday today, but you know we're good for it."

Alf thought about the visit he had been paid by Bluff Luton and Will Milam, and he quickly figured that there was some connection between their business and this mob of cowboys without any money on payday. He set up the drinks and moved in close to Joe for some conversation.

"Joe," he said, keeping his voice low, "what's going on?"

"Ain't nothing going on. We just didn't get paid today like we was supposed to, but we still got a powerful thirst."

"Come on," said Alf. "You can tell me the truth. Bluff Luton and Will Milam was in here talking to me about the papers on the ranch. Did Will Milam put you boys up to something?"

"I ain't seen Mr. Milam for a long time," said Joe. "Curly come out to see me last night."

"What'd he say?"

Joe thought about the wisdom of keeping his mouth shut, but he was enjoying Alf's credit, and he had probably already said too much. He might as well tell the whole story.

"Just for us to get off the ranch today without going for our pay. That's all."

"I knew it," said Alf. "Then Curly's with them. They're riding out to take the ranch back for Will, Joe. That's what they're up to."

"Do you think they can do it?"

"I don't know. There's those five detectives."

"Not anymore," said Joe. "Curly said they already killed two of them."

"Damn. I don't know," said Alf. "I don't know. They just might pull it off. Listen, Joe. You boys might ought to stick around for a while. We just might need to hold court here later. I might need to get out my justice of the peace coat and hold court. Yes, sir. Here. Let's have another round."

Harlan Bass lashed at his tired horse while the weak animal struggled to get a foothold on the slippery bank of the Red River. Behind him, his brother sat impatiently in the saddle, water up to his thighs.

"Well, hurry it on up, Harlan," said Odie. "While you're fooling around up there, I'm just asetting here getting soaked in this cold water. Hurry up."

"Shut up, Odie. Just shut up."

Harlan lashed some more, and the horse finally got a foot

on more or less solid ground. With a sudden lurch that almost
threw Harlan backward out of the saddle, he moved up onto
the bank. Odie followed, having almost as much trouble getting out of the river as had his brother.

"I don't see why we couldn't a tuck a ferry or something,"
said Odie. "I'm all wet. Probably going to get sick."

"Shut up, Odie."

The brothers rode a little ways up from the river's edge
and dismounted. Soon they had gathered a great pile of dry
brush and built themselves a fire which was much bigger than
their needs. They pulled off their boots and their trousers and
waved them over the flames in an attempt to dry them out.

"What do we do now, Harlan?" said Odie.

"Get our clothes dry, you dummy."

"That ain't what I meant. I know we got to get our clothes
dry. What I meant is what are we going to do after that? Are
we going to the Jessup ranch?"

Harlan was waving his boots over the fire, but in his impatience, he waved a little too close and burned his hand. He
yelped and tossed his boot into the air. Odie guffawed.

"Shut up, Odie," said Harlan. "Just shut up. Damn. That
hurt."

He retrieved his boot and set it along with the other one
on the ground close to the fire.

"We're going to get our clothes dry," he said, "then we're
going to find us something to eat, then we're going to look
for that damned Luton. Ain't no sense in going to the Jessups
without we've killed Luton. They're the stingiest bastards in
Texas. They ain't going to give us nothing for nothing. We
got to kill Luton first, but first we got to find him."

Sergeant Bluff Luton and Will Milam were waiting in front
of the Cross Timbers with their horses when Curly Wade
rode up to meet them. They climbed into their saddles.

"You ready?" said Luton.

"I'm ready," said Curly. He shot a quick glance at Milam.

"Why are you packing that scatter-gun?" he asked. "We ain't going to be able to get that close."

"You never know," said Milam. "I got my saddle gun here, too."

"You have extra shells?" asked Luton.

"Yeah," said Milam.

Curly patted the big pocket in the side of his jacket.

"I got enough here to go to war with," he said.

"All right," said Luton, "let's ride."

From a window on the second floor of the Cross Timbers, Emily Fisher watched as the three rode down the street on their way out of town. As they vanished from her sight, she pulled Matt close to her side and hugged him tightly. Across the street, nearly hidden around the corner of a building, Oliver Colfax puffed on a cigarette. As the riders disappeared, he casually stepped out into the street.

"I can't take much more of this waiting," said Toad Jessup as he sliced the end off his plug. He stuffed the slice into his mouth. "I just don't know how much more I can stand. You know, I'm kindly nervous in my stomach these days."

"What else can we do?" asked Jasper. "All we can do is just wait. We can't send anyone out to get more help. If we was to do that they might show up while he's gone. We need to keep everybody here. How much more nervous would your guts get if we sent somebody out of here?"

"Where are those damn drovers?" said Toad. "They're usually here by this time, just aclambering for their pay. Why are they late? The very time we need them around here and they're late. Where the hell are they?"

"Just keep your damn britches on," said Jasper. "They'll show up here pretty soon. Hell, it's payday. They'll be here. Then we can make them stay around while we send Jordan and them out to kill Luton. That's what we can do."

"Where the hell are they?"

* * *

Out on the front porch, Jordan Bradley saw the shapes of three riders appear on the horizon directly ahead. He tossed his cigarette away, and hefted the heavy revolver which hung at his side.

"Hey," he said.

At the other end of the porch, Simpson sat in a straight chair leaning back against the front wall of the house, balanced on two legs. He leaned forward, dropping the chair onto all fours.

"What?"

"There they are," said Bradley.

Simpson stood up and reached for the rifle which he had left standing against the porch rail. He chambered a shell.

"Hold it," said Bradley.

"You want to let the Jessups know?"

"Not just yet. I just now had a thought."

"Yeah?"

"You know that reward the Jessups offered for Luton?"

"Yeah."

"How we going to handle that?"

"I don't know," said Simpson.

"Run around back and get Rat Face," Bradley said. "I'll keep an eye on them out there. Bring Rat Face here. We need to talk."

Up on the rise, the three riders dismounted and each pulled a rifle out of a saddle boot. Luton could see the two men on the front porch, and he watched as one disappeared around the house and soon reappeared with a third man.

"What now?" said Curly.

"It looks like all three of our 'detectives' are out front now," said Luton. "The Jessups must be inside."

"So what do we do? Pick them off?"

"That's too long a shot," said Luton, "even for a Winchester. They know we're up here. They're caught with their pants down, you know. They were expecting all those cowboys. Let's just wait a bit and see what they do."

Just then the three men on the porch went into the house. Will Milam hawked and spat.

"They must be going to have a war council," he said.

"What the hell are you doing in here?" said Toad. "You're supposed to be out there watching. All three of you in here at once. Damn. Ain't nobody watching. Get back out there. They could just ride up here and walk right in on us. Kill us all."

"Just take it easy, Mr. Jessup," said Bradley. "Ain't no need to watch. They're here."

"What?"

Both Jessups ran to the window and crowded against each other trying to get a look.

"Straight ahead," said Bradley. "Up on the rise."

"Goddamn," said Toad.

"Three of them," said Jasper. "Well," he added, turning on the three range detectives, "what are you going to do?"

"That all depends on you two," said Bradley.

"What do you mean?" said Toad. "Go out there and kill them."

"You put out a reward offer for that Luton. If we get him for you today, how you going to handle that? We got to divide it up among the three of us or what?"

"You trying to blackmail us out of more money?" said Jasper.

"Listen here," said Toad. "That reward was put out to keep Luton from ever getting here. He's here, so there ain't no more reward. We pay you to protect us here at home, so get out there and protect us. Kill those bastards. They're trespassing on our land."

"Mr. Jessup," said Bradley, "you was going to pay some range bum to just ambush Luton out on the trail somewhere. Probably shoot him in the back. No danger at all. They didn't get the job done. Now we got to face him square."

"Facing up to the man ought to be worth more than just bushwhacking him," said Simpson.

"Him and two more," added Rat Face with a sneer.

Jasper Jessup walked up to Bradley and looked him in the eyes.

"That there reward," he said, "was for someone not on the payroll if he was to kill Luton. You're already on the payroll. You're already paid to protect us. That's just doing your job—earning your pay. That's why you don't get no reward."

Toad was still standing at the window looking out at the three men on the hill. He could feel the shirt sticking to his back from the sweat.

"Jasper," he said, his voice quavering, "let's just go on ahead and pay them the reward. Huh? It ain't right, them being on the payroll and all, but, hell, let's just go on ahead and do it. All right? This here is a—a crisis. It's a crisis situation that we're in here. All right?"

"The same amount as was offered before?" said Bradley.

"Yeah," said Toad. "Same amount. Go on out there now and kill them."

Jasper paced the floor, thoughtfully rubbing the stubble on his face.

"Ought to be three times as much," said Bradley.

"What?" said Toad.

"There's three of them," said Simpson, "and three of us. Ought to be three times the money."

Jasper whirled around and pounded the wall with his fist.

"No," he shouted. "Hell, no. It ain't three times as much. It ain't nothing. You work for wages, goddamn it. I ain't going to be blackmailed by no hired hands. Now you want to keep your jobs, you get the hell out of here and do what you're by God hired for. Go on."

Bradley looked at Rat Face, then at Simpson. Each nodded as he exchanged the glance. Each slowly withdrew the six-gun hanging at his hip and thumbed back the hammer.

"Go on," said Toad. "Go get them."

Bradley and Simpson turned their guns on Toad. Rat Face aimed at Jasper.

"What is this?" said Jasper.

"No," said Toad. "No. Wait. We'll pay."

Rat Face pulled the trigger, sending a slug into Jasper's sternum. Before Jasper hit the floor, the other two fired into Toad's body. Jasper lay on the floor gurgling, his eyeballs rolling around stupidly. Toad was dead, one bullet having torn through his larynx, the other his heart. Rat Face stepped over to where Jasper gasped for breath. He took a careful and callous aim and fired into Jasper's forehead, just between the eyes.

"The bastards," said Simpson.

"Check their pockets," said Bradley. "See if they've got any money on them."

"What about the safe?" said Rat Face.

"We can't open it," said Bradley. "And if we don't want to fight them three out there, we better not take the time to try."

Luton and his companions on the hill heard the shots. They readied their rifles and waited, but no one appeared outside the house.

"What was that all about?" asked Milam.

"I don't know, Will," said Luton. "Just hold tight and watch the house."

Then Luton saw the front door open slowly. He waited. A man stepped out onto the porch, holding both his hands about shoulder high. Neither hand held a gun.

"Hold it," said Luton.

When no shot was fired, the man, keeping his hands up, walked to the end of the porch, stepped off, and walked toward the stables. Two more stepped out behind him, their hands up like his, and followed him. All three went inside the small building.

"What the hell are they up to?" said Curly.

"We'll know soon enough," said Luton.

Soon the three men rode out of the stables on horseback and in single file. They still held their hands up. They rode toward the three men on the hill. When they had moved to about half the distance from the stables to the hilltop, Luton stood up.

"Keep them covered, boys," he said. Then he began walking toward the riders. "Hold it right there," he said. The riders stopped. "One of you come ahead to talk."

Between where Simpson and Rat Face sat on their horses and where Milam and Curly waited on the slope, Luton met Bradley. Bradley was the first one to speak.

"We're riding out," he said, "the three of us."

"How come?" said Luton, his rifle trained on Bradley's chest.

"We ain't running," said Bradley. "Them Jessups was just too tight with their money. They wouldn't make it worth our while to fight you. If you agree, we're riding out and leaving this part of the country."

Luton studied Bradley's face for a few seconds. Then he glanced quickly at the other two range detectives. "What were those shots we heard?" he said.

"Oh, they wasn't nothing," said Bradley. "Can we go?"

"All right," said Luton, "but first you ride back down there and join your partners. I'm not turning my back on you to walk up the hill."

Bradley turned his horse and rode back to join the other two. Then Luton turned and trotted back to Milam and Curly. He faced Bradley and waved his rifle.

"They're pulling out," he said.

"What for?" asked Milam.

"Said the Jessups was too tight."

"It might be a trick," said Curly.

"That's right," said Luton. "So watch them."

Milam watched the house while Curly watched the three riders. Luton, acting like the commander, glanced back and forth from one to the other. When the riders had finally gotten nearly out of sight, Luton spoke again.

"Curly," he said, "mount up and follow them a ways. Make sure they're doing what they said."

Curly climbed into his saddle and followed the three range detectives.

"What do we do?" said Milam.

"Wait."

A cool breeze had begun to blow across the barren hilltop. Luton noticed that his fingers were beginning to get cold holding the Winchester. He dropped it back into his saddle boot and rubbed his hands together.

"You suppose it's finally decided to turn winter down here?" he said.

"Yeah, it might," said Milam.

"You ought to come up north sometime," said Luton. "See a real winter. I've been in snow in Iowa up to my nipples."

"I don't want to go to no country where it snows higher than my boot tops."

It was about an hour before Curly came riding back. He pulled his horse up beside the other two and dismounted.

"Any action?" he said.

"No," said Luton, "it's damned quiet down there. What did you find out?"

"They rode on. Looks like they're playing it straight with us."

"All right," said Luton. "Let's move in on them. Will, you go over there and work your way along that fence line. Curly, head off over there to the right and ease in toward the house. I'm going straight at it from here. Be careful."

Luton moved slowly, watching the door and the windows of the house as he walked. It took a long time for him to reach the house, and even as he stepped up onto the porch, he expected shots to be fired. There was nothing. He eased up to the side of the door, which still stood open from when the three detectives had left the house, not bothering to close it. Still nothing happened. Luton leaned his rifle against the side of the house and slipped the Starr out of his holster. Then he quickly stepped inside.

* * *

Will Milam had seen Luton go inside the house, and when he heard no shots, he worried. He looked off to the other side of the house and caught the eye of Curly. Waving frantically at Curly, Milam stood and charged the house. He got to the porch before Curly and ran inside. There stood Luton in the middle of the floor. The Jessups were lying in grotesque and bloody heaps on the floor to either side of him. Luton looked stunned. He still held his revolver in his hand. He said nothing to Will Milam. Curly came inside and stopped.

"It's all over," he said.

"Yeah," said Milam, "and we didn't fire a shot."

Luton shook himself out of his daze and reholstered the Starr. "Welcome home, Will," he said. Then he turned and walked out the door.

Chapter Seventeen

The place was a mess, but it could be cleaned up. Will Milam was satisfied. He was back on his own ranch, in his own house. He had anticipated legal difficulties even after the Jessups were no longer a problem, but as things had turned out, that had not been the case. The legalities had been handled smoothly and without any hitches. The money that had been discovered in the house, well, the court had said that it could only assume that it was ranch money—money made by ranch operations—and, therefore, it went with the ranch. It belonged to Milam. As things turned out, Milam had not lost anything except a few years of time and frustration. There was at least as much money as he would have made had he been operating the ranch for himself all that time. Of course, he doubted that the money had all been honestly made by the Jessups, but there was no proof of that. The money was his. Everything had worked out all right, thanks to Bluff Luton.

God, it had been good to see Bluff again. Milam was disappointed that he had once again failed to convince Luton to stay on with him in Texas as a partner. He had thought that maybe this time it would work. This time Luton had a reason he could use to overcome his damned pride. He, after

147

all, had been the one who had gotten the ranch back for
Milam. But that hadn't been enough. Milam figured that
Texas just held too many painful memories for Luton. Maybe
when the ranch was all cleaned up, when Milam had set
everything back in order, maybe he would take a train ride
up to Iowa to visit old Bluff. Yeah. That would be the thing
to do.

He walked through the house, taking note of the stains
against the walls and on the floors where Toad Jessup had
spat his tobacco juice. He felt his stomach turn at the filth.

"It's a goddamned pigsty," he said out loud.

He would not move in just yet. No. He would stay in town
a bit longer and hire someone to come out and clean the
house. Then he would hire painters to cover the whole thing—
inside and out. He would buy new furnishings, have them
installed, and then he would move himself back into his
house. He would not move into the squalor the Jessups had
left behind. He felt a craving deep in his lungs for fresh air,
and he turned suddenly and strode to the front door.

He stopped abruptly when he stepped out onto the porch.
A man sat on a horse just in front of him. A man calm but
dangerous in appearance. A man Milam knew by sight and
by reputation.

"Milam," said the man by way of greeting.

"You're Colfax," said Milam.

"That's right. I want to talk to you."

"Not here."

Milam got his horse, and the two men rode together into
Wichita Falls. Milam picked a table in a corner of Church's
Saloon, away from all other customers. He bought a bottle
of good brandy, got two glasses from the bar, and sat down
with Colfax.

"What do you want with me?" he asked, pouring a drink
and shoving it across the table toward Colfax.

"I need some information."

"You worked for the Jessups, didn't you?"

"I don't work for anybody but myself. I'm a professional.

I agreed to do one job for the Jessups for a price. It never got done. They were killed first. They're nothing to me.''

Milam looked at Colfax. This was a professional killer. The job to which he referred so casually had been, Milam was almost certain, to kill Luton. But the Jessups were dead and Luton was gone. What did this man want? Was there any harm in talking to him? He tossed down his brandy and poured himself another, leaving the bottle in the middle of the table so that Colfax could help himself.

''All right,'' he said. ''What kind of information, Colfax?''

''I need to know about Bluff Luton. You know him.''

''I knew Bluff twenty years ago,'' said Milam, ''when we were both snot-nosed kids. I haven't seen him in years until he showed up here just the other day.''

''What about the Jessups?''

''What about them?''

''Did they know him?''

''Same as me,'' said Milam, tossing down another shot of brandy. ''Years ago.''

''Then that's what I want to know about,'' said Colfax. He put both elbows on the table and leaned toward Milam. Milam rolled the glass between his fingers and stared at it.

''I don't know, Colfax,'' he said. ''You know, Bluff Luton's a friend of mine, and I think that the Jessups hired you to kill him.''

''I won't deny it,'' said Colfax, ''but I'm not admitting anything either. But what if they did? I had a hundred chances to kill Luton if I'd wanted to kill him, and I never tried it. Never. Did you ever hear that I tried to kill him?''

''No.''

''The Jessups are dead. I don't work for free, and even if I was trying to kill him, what I want to know from you wouldn't help me any.''

''All right,'' said Milam. ''What do you want to know?''

''I've just got one question. Why? The Jessups wanted Luton killed in a real bad way. It seems as if they sent word up to him that they were here so that he would head down this way. Then they put a bounty on his head. Why did they want him killed after all these years? Why? And when Luton heard they were here, he dropped everything and came after them. Why? Why did he want them so badly? That's all I want to know, Milam. Why?''

Milam poured two more brandies. He heaved a long sigh.

"Colfax," he said, "back when Wichita Falls was just a trading post—wasn't nothing else here—I was hanging around this part of the country. I was just a gangly legged kid, couldn't read or write. Still can't. I'd never done nothing but punch cows. I wasn't too smart, but even I was smart enough to know that I'd never get rich punching someone else's beef. I had a couple of bucks in my pockets, and I had an idea. I wanted to build up my own spread. Right here. Right up here along the Red River. I had the clothes on my back and my saddle and pony. I knew what I wanted, but I had no idea yet how I was going to get it."

Milam leaned back and took a sip of brandy. Colfax could sense that this was going to be a long story, so he settled comfortably into his chair. Milam put down his glass and continued the tale.

"Well, like I said, there wasn't nothing at Wichita Falls except that old trading post, but it was a place where folks tended to congregate. There was a big horse race planned. Entry fees was charged so that a purse could be offered to the winner, and then there was side bets—some of them pretty substantial. Bluff Luton and his little brother, Bud, happened along just then. Bud had himself a good horse, and he thought that he could win that race. Bluff decided to let him run, even though he thought that it was against his better judgment. He wanted to keep moving. They was in about the same financial shape as me, and they was heading for the big ranches up in Indian Territory. Just looking for cowboy jobs. We got acquainted. Somehow me and Bluff just seemed to hit it off. You know how that sometimes happens."

Colfax thought with mild irritation that indeed he did know

how that sometimes happens. It must be something about Luton, he thought. What the hell was it about that man anyway? He glanced up at Milam and realized that here was another man he was beginning to like. His thoughts bothered him, so he pushed them aside roughly, somewhere into the back of his mind. He needed to concentrate on the story just now anyhow. Milam was still talking.

"I tried to talk him out of the Indian Territory notion," he said. "Tried to talk him into staying around these parts and throwing in with me as a partner, but he wouldn't go for it. Said I'd wind up going busted. Funny thing is, I did lose my ranch, and he had to come back and save it for me. But that's getting ahead of the story."

He took another sip of his brandy.

"It seems to me like Bluff just didn't have no ambition. All he wanted was just a job. He's still like that. Hell, I just offered him half of the place if he'd stay on."

Colfax's brows rode up on his forehead at that news.

"Just now, I mean," said Milam. "Since he got it back for me, you know? He turned me down flat. Headed back for his little town marshal's job. No ambition."

Milam slumped back in his chair. He looked to Cole as if he were lost in his memories. He looked old. Colfax knew that he and Luton and Milam were all about the same age, yet Milam looked old. From building up a ranch and then losing it? From twenty years of loneliness? From a lost friendship? Friendship. It was a word that seldom occurred to Colfax. He looked at Milam and thought of Luton as he refilled the glasses and shoved Milam's drink toward him.

"Go on," he said.

Milam took the drink and sipped it. Then he set the glass down on the table in front of him and stared into the brown liquid.

"They stayed around for the race," he said. "That race drawed a bunch of people in. They come from all around. Some of them come to race, some come to bet, some just come to watch. There was a bunch of Chickasaw Indians from up in the Territory racing their ponies, and a few Choc-taws. There was people from all over Texas, some from New Mexico. Hell, they come from all over. That's when the Jes-sups come in. We thought that we was poor. Hell, these two was in rags. They was dirty. They stunk. They went around begging smokes or chews, begging food, begging drinks, begging money. They tried to get in card games on credit. They got themselves beat up a time or two. It didn't seem to slow them down none. The kind that can't seem to take a hint.''

He sipped his brandy again.

"I didn't want to have nothing to do with them, but Bluff was softhearted. He wouldn't run them off. He'd talk civil to them when they come around, so they got to hanging around a lot. Watching Bud run that smart horse of his. Did I tell you about that horse?''

He glanced up at Colfax, who didn't bother to answer, having figured that the question was a rhetorical one. Sure enough, Milam continued.

"Sandy Anna,'' he said, and he chuckled and shook his head. "That Bud. Named his horse Sandy Anna. Course all of us Texans got a kick out of that. He called her Sandy for short. A dun she was with a black mane and tail. Real pretty, and Bud kept her groomed up real nice. He'd work her, but he wouldn't work her too hard. She was a fine animal, as fine as I've ever seen, and she tuck to Bud same as he tuck to her.''

Milam suddenly looked self-conscious. He shook his head a little as if trying to shake off some reverie. Then he downed his brandy.

"This story's taking too long to tell,'' he said.

"I got time,'' said Colfax, "and you got all my atten-tion.''

He refilled Milam's glass and pulled the makings out of his pocket.

"Smoke?'' he said.

"Don't mind if I do,'' said Milam.

Colfax tossed the makings across the table. Milam resumed his tale as he rolled himself a smoke.

"Well," he said, "I'll try to make it short. Them Jessups said they'd bet everything they had on Bud and Sandy to win. We knew that was just talk. They didn't have nothing to bet. They did have guns. That seemed to be all they had. Well, Bud won that race. I never seen a race like that one in my life, not before or since. There was a bunch of horses in it. I don't know how many, but there was a bunch. And they was all good, too. But that horse that Bud Luton had—damn. It was something else. And that boy rode like the wind. He won it clear and clean. There wasn't a single protest. Not one. The closest thing behind him was a Chickasaw from just up across the river riding on a pinto."

He stopped talking to lick the paper on his cigarette, then picked up a match off the table and struck it. As he lit his smoke, Colfax retrieved the makings and began to roll one for himself.

"They got the prize money and packed up to head north," said Milam, exhaling a cloud of smoke. "I couldn't try to talk them into staying with me no more, because if I had, it would of looked like I wanted to use their money to get my ranch started. I hated to see them go. Most of the crowd tuck off right after the race was done, but there was still some of us hanging around the Falls.

"Next morning I was in the trading post talking with the trader there about the race, just passing the time wondering what my next move would be, when a cowboy come puffing in. I'd seen him around, but I didn't know him by name. He said that someone had stole his two horses sometime in the night. He was left afoot. He needed a horse to go after them. The trader didn't have no horses. His business had been real good while there was so many people around. The cowboy turned on me.

" 'You got a good horse and saddle,' he said.

" 'Yeah,' I said, 'and I aim to keep them.'

" 'Ain't you the fella that's been running around here talking about how you aim to start a big ranch of your own?' he said.

" 'That's my plan,' I said, 'and that's why I need my good horse.'

" 'You got any land?' he said.

"I had to own that I didn't, and that I didn't have enough money to buy myself any either.

" 'Well,' he said, reaching into his pockets and pulling out a whole mess of paper, 'I've got these old land certificates. They're still good, and there's still plenty of public-domain land around here. I'll trade you some of these for your horse and saddle.'

" 'My horse and saddle's worth maybe thirty dollars, mister,' I said. 'What am I going to do with thirty dollars' worth of land and no horse?'

"Well, he paced back and forth across the floor for a mite, and then he turned on me again, and I thought that he was going to whip me right then and there.

" 'Listen,' he said, 'I've been carrying these damn things around for too long. I got no intention of settling down anywhere anyhow, and right now I'm desperate for a horse. I'll give you the whole damn mess for your horse and saddle.'

" 'How much you talking about?' I said.

" 'Twelve hundred acres' worth,' he said, and he slapped them certificates down on the counter. Well, that put me in an embarrassing position. That's a good chunk of land. With that much land, maybe I could find a way to get myself another horse and then some cattle. That would be the start that I needed. I'd heard of land certificates, but I'd never seen one, and I didn't know that they were still in use. What's more, I couldn't read."

Milam looked down at the table as if he were ashamed.

"Still can't," he said. "I either had to let the opportunity pass me by or admit my ignorance. I decided to swallow my pride and ask Alf—that's the traders name, you know. He's still there. I decided to ask Alf for some help. He examined the certificates for me and told me that they were genuine as far as he could tell. And they did total up to twelve hundred acres' worth. They had been issued some years back, and the state was no longer putting them out, but them that had been issued and never put to use was still good.

" 'That's a hell of a lot of land for a horse and saddle, mister,' I said.

" 'Do we have a deal?' he said.

"Well, I tuck him up on it, so there I was with no horse and no saddle, with about twenty bucks to my name and twelve hundred acres' worth of Texas land certificates. The cowboy tuck off right away."

Milam took a final drag off his cigarette, dropped the butt to the floor, and ground it with his boot.

"I spent the next couple of days," he said, "with Alf's help, figuring how to turn my certificates into land. It wasn't easy, since I was stuck afoot and since I can't read, but he wrote some letters for me to send into the state, and he helped me identify some public-domain land, and things was looking up for me. Then the cowboy came back. He had his two horses and two more in addition to mine which he was still riding. I watched him ride up to the trading post, and then I recognized them two extra horses.

" 'What happened?' I said. 'Where'd you get them horses? Them's the Lutons' horses. Bluff and Bud.'

"He told me to slow down and let him get out of the saddle and get a drink. I did, and we went inside. Finally he told me the whole story. He had caught up with the horse thieves up in the Chickasaw Nation. They was camped down in a draw, and he had tried to sneak up on them, but they had got wind of him. They had exchanged a few shots, then the two thieves had hightailed it out of there. He thought that he had winged one of them, and he thought about giving chase but decided against it. One of them was shot, and they had left the horses. That was enough. Besides, his mount was tired. He had his horses back. He thought that he recognized the two extra horses that they had left behind, so he decided to bring them along back to the post in case their owners showed up looking for them. He hadn't got a real good look at the horse thieves, but from the way he described them, I thought that it sounded like those Jessups.''

Milam stopped talking. His head sagged onto his chest. Colfax thought that the man looked tired—old and tired. And telling this story, recalling these events from his past, was painful to him. He picked up the bottle and refilled Milam's glass, then offered the makings to Milam again. Milam took them and began rolling himself another smoke.

"Well," he said, taking a deep breath, "I told him again whose horses those two extras were, and he decided that he would ride out with me to see if we could find out anything about the Lutons. It didn't take us long. It was just up by the Red River near the crossing into the Chickasaw Nation that we found them. We found one grave, and we figured that it must be Bud, because we also found Bluff there. He was more dead than alive. We hauled him back to the Falls and patched him up the best we could, and the cowboy decided to head on back toward south Texas. I was afraid that he'd want his land certificates back, but he didn't. In fact, he asked me if I wanted my horse and saddle back, and he sold them back to me for my last twenty dollars. I never seen him again.

"It was several days before Bluff seemed like he might live and before he could talk and tell us what had happened. Bluff and Bud had headed north after the race with their winnings in their pockets. They had got as far as the Red River crossing. There's a lot of brush there, you know. Bluff was riding ahead, and from just ahead in the brush a shot was fired. He seen it coming, but too late. It hit him in the chest and knocked him out of the saddle. Bud jumped off his horse and run to see about his big brother. Bluff couldn't see much. He was only about half conscious. He wanted Bud to run, but he couldn't seem to say anything. Then he seen the Jessups out of the brush over Bud's shoulder. Bud must of heard them, because he stood up and turned just as Toad Jessup fired a shotgun blast into Bud's chest. Then they kicked

Bluff in the head and he went out. He woke up later and managed to bury Bud's body by digging in the ground with his bare hands and by piling up rocks. Then he passed out again, and he didn't regain consciousness until after he'd been back at the trading post for several days. After we'd found him and brought him back.

"I told him how we'd happened to find him. Told him we had his horses back. When he was able to get around—he wasn't nowhere near healthy yet—but when he could get around again, he got up and got ready to go after them Jessups. I tried to talk him out of it, but he wouldn't listen. All he could think about was killing them Jessups. He gave me Bud's horse. Said all he needed was one. Then he took off, and I never seen him again until just this time. Twenty years later. I don't know how long he hunted them Jessups before he give it up. All I know is that a few years back I started hearing stories about him. He made himself quite a reputation as a lawman. Then it seems that he kind of settled down in that little town up in Iowa. That was the last I knew until he came back. I guess that's about it."

Milam leaned heavily back in his chair. He felt very old and very tired.

"Not quite," said Colfax.

"Huh?"

"What about the Jessups?"

"Oh, yeah. Like I said, I don't know how long Bluff hunted them two or when he finally gave it up. When I started hearing stories about him being a lawman and such, I kind of figured that he had probably got them and got it out of his system and settled down to a career as a lawman. If you can call that settling. I'd hear about him cleaning up one little town and then another, so I never really knew just where he was at. Only where he had been last. I figured he had caught up with them. Until I seen them again."

"When was that?"

"Just a little while after the war. They come back into these parts. I seen them over at Henrietta. I went to the law

and told them about what them two had done. I told them
that they had murdered young Bud Luton, but the court said
that all it had to go on was hearsay evidence. I couldn't even
produce Bluff to testify, and even then it would just have been
his word against that of the Jessups. The whole thing had
happened so many years ago that there wouldn't be much
chance of coming up with any real evidence.

"Besides that, the Jessups had some friends in the carpet-
bagger government. You know how things were in Texas
after the war. So nothing come of it, and I didn't know where
to find Bluff. After enough time went by, I just kind of put
it out of my mind, but I guess the Jessups didn't. They come
after me. Not to kill me. Just to break me.

"They went to the court about two years ago with a document they said that I had signed. I can't write, you know,
but it had a mark on it they said was my mark, and it was
signed by six witnesses. I swore and be damned that I hadn't
signed no papers, but it was my word against eight. The court
said that I had sold my ranch to them two."

"That tells me everything except how the Jessups found
out Luton was in Riddle, Iowa, and how he found out they
were back here."

"About a month ago we got a copy of a newspaper from
Dallas. It had a story in it about a little town called West
Riddle in Nebraska. It was about how a new town marshal
in West Riddle had cleaned out a den of thieves up there.
The writer said that the only thing that puzzled him was how
a den of thieves could operate so long just across the river
from Riddle, Iowa, where the town marshal was the famous
Bluff Luton. Then I knew where Bluff was at, and I guess
the Jessups seen the same paper, or like me, heard folks
talking about the story.

"I guess that just hearing his name again made them nervous. They was beginning to be prominent citizens around
here. They was landowners. With stolen land, but landowners still. If they'd heard of him, he might hear about them. I
guess they just decided that they'd try to get him first before

he caught up with them by surprise someday. They sent word up, using my name, that they was here.''

Colfax rolled himself a cigarette and lit it. He took a deep draw and exhaled the smoke.

'' 'Othello's occupation's gone,' '' he said.

"What?"

"Oh, nothing, Mr. Milam. Nothing. That Sarge is a hell of a man.''

"Yes, he is. Is there anything else I can tell you?"

"No. I think you've answered all my questions. Thank you for your time.''

Colfax stood up as if to leave.

"I guess old Sarge is on his way back to Ioway by now,'' he said.

"Not just yet," said Milam. "He's going to Boston first."

"Boston?"

"That's right."

"Well," said Colfax, extending his hand, "thanks again. Be seeing you.''

As he walked out the door and climbed onto his horse, Colfax was thinking about Bluff Luton. Gone to Boston. Goddamn him. There can only be one reason for him to do that. That damn fool. Gone to Boston. Well, he ain't even to Henrietta yet. He's got to get there first to catch the train.

Inside the saloon, Will Milam took another sip of brandy. He wondered why he had volunteered that last bit of information to Colfax. That Luton had gone to Boston. Nothing else he had told Colfax could have helped the killer if he still meant to assassinate Luton. But that last could. Why had he told the man? Colfax hadn't even asked for that information. He had said that Milam had answered all his questions, and he was leaving. Then Milam had blurted out that Luton was going to Boston. Damn, he thought. Colfax had gotten him off guard, had made him comfortable. He had talked for so long about Bluff Luton that he had just kept going without thinking. He cursed himself, then poured another drink. Ah, hell, he thought, he ain't going after him. The Jessups is dead. Why would he want to kill Bluff now? There's nobody to pay him for it. He ain't going after him.

He tossed down the brandy. Soon he would be drunk. Tomorrow he would hire someone to clean up his house. He thought about Bluff Luton riding alone toward Henrietta, and he wondered which direction Colfax had taken out of town.

"No," he said out loud, "he ain't going after him."

Chapter Eighteen

Luton wanted to get this last trip over and done and get back to the peace and quiet of Riddle, Iowa, but he didn't yet want to get on the train. He didn't want to deal with the rowdy crowds of Henrietta again. It would take a little longer, he knew, but he would ride horseback across the Red River and into the Choctaw Nation. He would catch the train up there. He wanted some time to himself. Texas weather was unpredictable as always, and now it was amazingly warm for this time of year. Luton knew that the farther north he went, the colder it would get. He wondered how much snow awaited him in Riddle, but it would be awhile before he would find out, and right now it was warm. He rode toward the Red River, and he thought about this one last task he had set for himself. He would send Will Milam some money to pay him back for the rail ticket. He would do that. Will was okay now, and Emily and Matt—they would be, too. All in all, it had been a worthwhile trip. It had turned out to be much more than he had bargained for, and he was glad of that. Suddenly Luton stopped his horse. Two riders were approaching from up ahead. He hefted the Starr to make sure it was sliding easily in its holster.

The two were in no hurry. When they finally rode up to within earshot, Luton spoke.

"Howdy, strangers," he said.

The riders halted their sorry-looking ponies and climbed wearily out of their worn saddles. The older appearing of the two seemed to be about thirty years old. He had unruly, sandy hair and needed a shave. The other was maybe twenty-five and equally as unkempt. Their clothing was ordinary, though threadbare and dirty. They didn't have the look of cowboys. The older, and shorter, of the two had a six-gun in a holster tied down to his leg. The other had one tucked into the waistband of his trousers. The older one spoke to Luton.

"You traveling far?"

"Far enough," said Luton.

"I'm Harlan Bass, and this here's my little brother, Odie. We been on the road a long time. We're broke and hungry. You got any food on you?"

Luton didn't like the looks of these two, but they did look hungry and poor. He had some hardtack and jerky in his roll. He could spare some. He climbed down out of the saddle.

"I can spare a little," he said, reaching into his roll.

"You a cowboy?"

"Nope," said Luton.

"Just traveling through?"

"Yeah," said Luton. He reached out toward the nearest of the two with some jerky. "Here."

"Jerky. That all you got? Odie, all he's got is jerky."

Luton took a couple of easy steps backward. He had one of these road thugs on either side of him. He silently cursed himself for allowing that to happen. He had been caught off guard—tricked into thinking that they were just beggars. He should have known better, but he realized that with the Jessups and their hired killers out of the way, he was already beginning to relax again.

"I've got some hardtack in here," he said, reaching for the roll behind the saddle again.

"Hardtack," said Odie.

"Well," said Luton, "you want it or not?"

He tossed the jerky at Harlan and the hardtack toward Odie, and as they reached automatically to catch it, he jerked out his Starr.

"Now," he said, "I think you two boys just wore out your welcome. Pick up that food. I hate to see good food go to waste. Pick it up and ride on your way."

Harlan and Odie Bass both bent over to pick up what they had failed to catch. They stuffed the food into their coat pockets, Odie first taking a bite of the hardtack.

"Now mount up," said Luton, "and ride out."

The Bass brothers climbed onto their horses, but Harlan, thinking that his right hand was hidden from Luton's view, reached for his six-gun. As he turned to point it at Luton, Luton's Starr roared. The bullet struck Harlan's gun hand in the heel of his palm, tore through the length of the forearm, and ripped out at the elbow. Harlan bellowed in pain and horror as he clutched at the wretched-looking forearm in a futile attempt to staunch the gushing blood. Odie had pulled out his pistol, but it was pointed at the ground. He needed to thumb back the hammer, and he needed to swing it up to point it at Luton. He stood frozen, his young face a picture of indecision.

"Try it, young fella," said Luton. "I'll scatter your damned brains all over north Texas."

"No. No. Don't shoot," said Odie, dropping his gun. "My brother's hurt. I got to help him."

"Load him up and get the hell out of here," said Luton.

"Damn you, Luton," said Harlan.

Odie was moving toward Harlan, but Luton stopped him.

"Hold on," he said. "You know me. How come?"

"We don't know you," said Odie.

"You can stand there and deny it until your brother bleeds to death."

"Tell him, Odie," whined Harlan. "Tell him. I'm hurting here."

"Well, all right," said Odie. "Yeah. We knew who you was."

"How do you know me?"

"We seen you before."

"Where?"

"Goddamn it, Odie. Tell him."

"All right. All right. We was with Randall Lee Bow whenever you killed him by that water tower—him and Joe Don Tucker. We was there."

"Oh," said Luton, recalling the incident, "the two that got away."

"That's right," said Odie. "Now can we go?"

"Were you sent by the Jessups to do that job on me?"

"Yeah, the Jessups. That's right. Now can we go?"

"Why were you laying for me today?"

"Well," said Odie, "the same reason, I guess. We need some money, and the Jessups is paying."

"You just get back from up north?"

"Yeah."

"Well, you two drag yourselves on into Henrietta, and you'll find out that you damn near got yourselves killed today for nothing. The Jessups are dead. There's no one left to pay up if you did kill me. Now get out."

Luton sent a shot between Odie's feet, and Odie jumped straight up into the air with a squeal. He ran to his crying brother and helped him to mount up, then climbed onto his own nag and hurried off, leaving Harlan to follow in his dust as best he could. Luton fired again over their heads to speed Harlan on his way. He stood and watched them for a long moment. How many more? he wondered. How many more ain't got the word yet?

Oliver Colfax was in a hurry, but he knew that he had to pace himself carefully. First of all, he had to watch the trail he was following. If he got in too much of a hurry, he could lose it before he realized what had happened. Then, too, he had to think about his horse. It wouldn't do him any good to get somewhere faster with a worn-out mount. But the main thing was that his years of experience as a manhunter had taught him never to rush into anything. Hurrying made men careless, and being careless got people killed. He was anxious, but he kept the reins on himself. He took his time. He made sure. And that gave him time to think.

He knew that Luton had a railroad ticket, so he figured that the marshal would ride horseback over to Henrietta to catch the train. But the trail wasn't heading for Henrietta. It was heading almost due north, toward the Red River, the Choctaw Nation. What the hell was Luton up to anyway? Well, he would find out. Patience always paid off in the end.

Harlan and Odie Bass were camped alongside the Wichita River not far from where Sergeant Bluff Luton had shot Harlan and run them off. Harlan's mangled arm was wrapped tightly in strips of rag torn from an old and soiled shirt. Dried blood was caked on the rags, and underneath it all, Harlan's arm was throbbing with pain. He lay on a dirty blanket, rolling from side to side and groaning. Odie sat beside a blazing campfire greedily devouring what was left of a Texas jackrabbit he had shot. Harlan had refused to eat. He was not squeamish over the jackrabbit, nor even at Odie's pathetic attempts at culinary art. He was nauseous with the pain in his arm. In fact, the pain was no longer just in his arm. It was beginning to shoot throughout his body.

"You don't think about nothing but your own self," he winced through his agony. "Just only your own goddamn belly."

"Got to eat," said Odie. "Man can't keep going without he eats."

"You could get me to a doctor and then find something to eat. What about me? Huh? What about me? I'm your brother. I could die right here and you dripping jackrabbit grease off your damn chin."

"Shut up. I offered you some, didn't I? You wouldn't take it, so I et it."

"I'm hurting too bad to eat. I need a doctor. I'll get some kind of putrefaction or gangrene or something without a doctor. Shit, you didn't do nothing for me."

"I put that there bandage on you, didn't I? Well, didn't I? Hell, you're the ungratefulest bastard I ever did see."

"You didn't do nothing but tear up one of my own shirts, of which I only got two in the first place, and wrapped it all around my arm. You didn't clean up the wound or nothing. Just wrapped it up and forgot about it. Couldn't use your own old shirt neither, could you? Had to use mine. You don't care nothing for me. Your own brother. Don't care nothing. If Mama could see us now . . ."

"Oh, hell, goddamn," shouted Odie, tossing the last bone away, "shut up. Let's get mounted up, and I'll find you a doc."

"Sure," said Harlan, "now that there ain't nothing more to eat. I coulda died already for all you care."

"Saddle up and let's get going."

"Saddle up? What the hell do you mean, 'Saddle up'? Just what the hell do you mean? I only got one good arm. I can't saddle no horse. I'm sick. You saddle up the horses, and then you help me up into the saddle. And when we get started, you go easy. I can't ride fast. You go easy and look out for me. Don't you go running off from me like you done before. You hear? Hell, I coulda fell off my horse and died back yonder, and you'd a never knowed. You never even looked back. Hell of a lot you care."

While this tirade was going on, Odie had managed to saddle both nags. He led his brother's mount over to where the wounded man still lay on the ground.

"Quit your bellyaching and get on up here," he said.

With much groaning and wincing, Harlan stood up. He reached down for the blanket he had been lying on.

"Leave that old flea-infested rag just lay where it's at," said Odie. "Come on."

He helped Harlan up into the saddle, then went for his own mount.

"Which way we going?" said Harlan.

"Nearest town's thisaway."

Odie kicked the bony ribs of his sad old horse and started riding. He didn't look back.

"Hey," shouted Harlan, "there you go again. Goddamn it. Wait for me. I'm hurting back here. I can't keep up with you. Wait up. I ever see that son of a bitch Luton again, I'm going to tie him up naked and skin him alive. Damn it. Wait up."

Up ahead, as he was climbing up a rise from the bank of the Wichita, Odie halted his nag. As Harlan got closer, he shouted again at his brother.

"Well, you can move on now. I'm here. Don't set there all day."

Odie didn't answer, and he didn't move. Harlan started to yell again. Then he saw the rider blocking his brother's path. He rode slowly up beside Odie and stopped. He thought about their lost guns back there where they had met Luton.

"Howdy," he said.

"Well, if it isn't the famous Bass brothers."

Oliver Colfax was seated comfortably atop a large roan stallion, an 1866 model Winchester .44 carbine lying across the saddle in front of him.

"You're Colfax," said Harlan.

"That's right."

"My brother's hurt," said Odie.

"I got to have a doctor," whimpered Harlan.

"I take it you've encountered Sergeant Bluff Luton," said Colfax. "I'm dogging his trail. What shape is he in?"

The brothers looked at each other, then down at their battered saddle horns. Odie looked back up toward Colfax.

"Well," he said haltingly, "we seen him. Yeah. It was him that done this to my brother. He didn't give us a chance."

Colfax thought about Luton. If what Odie Bass said were true, both Bass brothers would be dead. Luton was remaining true to his character. He hadn't yet slipped up. These two obviously had tried to bushwhack Luton, and even so, Luton had not killed them. *Well*, he thought, *I'll do it for him.* He raised the Winchester and pointed it at Odie.

"Hey, don't," screamed Odie, slapping madly for the spot where his six-gun should have been.

Colfax pulled the trigger and sent a .44 slug into Odie's chest. Odie's body was flung backward in the saddle, but his feet were both caught in the stirrups. He fell straight back and lay ludicrously splayed out across the rump of his nag. Meanwhile, Harlan had been fumbling for his gun, though he knew that he didn't have one, and his mangled arm made him awkward and clumsy.

"Damn you," he shouted.

Colfax turned his barrel on Harlan and levered another shell into the chamber.

"Don't," said Harlan.

Colfax fired. The bullet knocked out four of Harlan's front teeth and tore a hole in the back of his skull. He fell down between the two nags, his brother's left arm slowly waving over him.

Chapter Nineteen

Luton rode slowly. His meeting with the Bass brothers had made him cautious once more, and he knew that he had allowed himself plenty of time. He was not going back to Henrietta to catch the train. He had seen enough of Texas rowdies to last him a good long while, and he wanted to be alone. He wanted to feel free and clean. He would take a leisurely ride up to and across the Red River and into the Choctaw Nation, and catch the train at Colbert's Ferry. Will Milam's business took him up in that direction often enough, he had told Luton, that he could pick up the horse later. He had given Luton the name of a man to leave the animal with until that time came. As he rode along, Luton found himself both looking over his shoulder frequently and scanning the horizon ahead of him carefully. He was fairly certain that he had seen the last of Oliver Colfax. The man only killed for money and had not come to grips with his own philosophical problems concerning Luton before his employers were dead. However, the Bass brothers had not heard of the Jessups' deaths, and there could be more like them running around loose yet. He didn't really think so, but his encounter with the Basses made him conscious of the possibility. Better be overly cautious than dead.

He glanced back again, at first casually, then fixing his
eyes on an emerging image on the far horizon. He squinted
to help bring the image into sharper focus. A rider. A rider
on his trail. Possibly on his trail. Maybe not. He watched for
a moment. The rider seemed to be headed directly for him,
but there was quite a distance between them, and the landscape was so flat and monotonous that Luton couldn't be
sure. He rode on, looking over his shoulder more regularly.
The rider seemed to be gaining on him. Luton was certain
then that the man was following him. He was still too far
away to see clearly—much too far to identify.

Back down the trail, Oliver Colfax cursed the north Texas
flatland which allowed his prey to see him coming from such
a distance. He didn't hurry. He kept a steady pace. He had
Luton in sight now, and Luton probably had no idea who
Colfax was. Luton may not even realize that he's being followed. Might think it's just some drifter up here. Take it easy.
Let him think that for a while. Let him wonder and worry.
Get his neck tired looking over his shoulder. Colfax noticed
that Luton didn't seem to be in a hurry either. Well, Cole
would just keep dogging the trail, slowly closing the gap.

Regularly Luton looked back over his shoulder to find the
man still there. He wondered who it could be. He could slow
down and let the rider get close enough to get a good look at
him. He rejected that idea. Besides, it seemed to him that
the man was shortening the distance between them without
his help. He didn't seem to be hurrying, but he did seem to
be getting closer. Closer. Yes. He seemed a bit closer each
time Luton looked back. There was something familiar about
the man. What was it? Who could he be? Something about
the horse, maybe, or the way the man sat the horse. If only
he were a little closer. It might not be anyone after him, but
then again, it might be someone else like those last two he
had run up against, another one who hadn't gotten the word.
Damn. He wondered how long after their deaths the Jessups

would continue to pursue him. He glanced back over his shoulder.

"The son of a bitch is following me," he said.

He looked around. There wasn't much relief from the bleak landscape, but off to his left there was a slight rise in the otherwise level ground. He turned his horse toward it.

"Come on," he said.

It put him on a western course, riding almost parallel to the river, not toward it, but he wanted to get something besides flat between him and that rider back there. He headed for the rolling space at a gallop, the distance between him and his pursuer widening slightly again. He couldn't tell as he headed for the easy rise what the rider in the distance was going to do about his direction of travel. As he topped the rise, Luton saw a mesquite thicket ahead to his right, and he turned his horse toward the thicket. Approaching the runty mesquite trees, he slowed his mount to a walk and eased into the shadows of the brush. *I'll just wait here a bit and see what he does,* he thought.

When Oliver Colfax lost sight of his prey over the rise, he felt a slight sense of panic in his breast, and he spurred his big roan. Upon achieving the rise, he pulled back on the reins. Luton was nowhere in sight.

"Damn it," he said as he scanned the horizon. He couldn't have gone far enough to be beyond the range of vision. The landscape was too flat. The slight rise which he had just topped and which had allowed Luton to evade him for the moment was the only relief from the monotony until well up close to the river. The mesquite thicket was a minor relief, and that was the only place Luton could be, Cole decided. So Luton had determined that he was being followed. Did he know who it was? Whether he did or not, it was a new game now. The prey knew that it was being stalked. Colfax climbed down out of the saddle and sat cross-legged in the dirt. He didn't know exactly what his next move would be. If he rode on down, Luton could pick him off easily before he could manage to locate him in the thicket. But would he? Would Luton pick a man off like that? He hadn't even killed those slimy Bass brothers when he had good reason. He stared into the thickness of mesquite.

"Damn pesky import," he said.

He could try to wait Luton out. He would have to leave that thicket sooner or later. Then the hot Texas sun reminded Colfax that his quarry could probably stand to wait in among the mesquite trees, as scrawny as they were, longer than he could stand it out there in the middle of nothing. The dirt on which he sat began to heat up his rump. He pulled a bandanna out of his pocket and mopped the sweat off his brow. Yes, Luton could easily wait him out. He had to think of something else.

"Hell of an excuse for winter," he said.

Down in the thicket, Bluff Luton watched the man dismount and squat in the dirt at the top of the rise, and he recognized Oliver Colfax. *So it's time,* he thought. *I might have known I'd not seen the last of him.* He knew that he was hidden from Colfax's view, and he knew that Colfax knew that he was somewhere in the thicket. He didn't know what the gunman would do next. If Colfax came closer, Luton could kill him before he could figure out where Luton was hidden. That was why he waited at the top of the rise. The distance was too great for a pistol shot. Luton pulled out his Starr and checked the load. He knew that Colfax had a rifle. His own Winchester was once again wrapped in the blanket roll and tied behind the saddle. Even if he could get it out without giving away his position, it would be too difficult to maneuver in the thicket. He would have to wait Colfax out. At least he had shade, and Cole was out in the sun. Then he noticed the dark, lowering clouds off to the west. They might not mean anything, but they looked to Luton like fast-moving storm clouds. "Coming this way," he said, and he made his way slowly and carefully to the side of the borrowed horse.

"Take it easy, big fella," he said.

He loosened the ties on his blanket roll and pulled off the yellow rain slicker in which it had been wrapped. He put on the slicker, then settled back down to watch Colfax. He reached to pull the collar up around his neck and felt a stabbing pain in his right hand. Damn. Mesquite thorns. He licked the blood off the back of his hand. The storm appeared more imminent, so he moved back to the horse to tie the reins to the branch of a scruffy tree.

Up on the rise, Colfax mopped his brow again. He stuffed the bandanna into his pocket, and he, too, saw the clouds menacing, gathering for their assault.

"That's about enough of this," he said, either to himself or to his horse. He stood up and slapped the dust off the seat of his pants. Moving to the roan, he slid his Winchester out of its sheath, maneuvered the roan around until it stood more or less parallel to the line of mesquites before him in the distance, then stepped behind the horse and laid the rifle across the saddle.

"Steady, old boy," he said, his voice calm and quiet. "Steady."

He fired a round into the thicket at its farthest end to his right. The roan snorted, shook its head, and stamped the dry, dusty ground.

"Steady," said Colfax. He moved the barrel slightly to the left and fired again.

The first shot startled Luton down in the thicket. He inched forward and squinted toward Colfax through the tangle of branches and thorns. *What the hell is he doing?* He held up the Starr as if he would return fire, but he knew that he would be wasting bullets to shoot back at this distance. He watched as Colfax fired his third shot. *So that's it,* he told himself. *He's going to sweep this thicket with rifle shots from one end to the other, hoping to get me with a chance shot, or else to spook me out of here.* A fourth rifle shot was fired. Luton knew that he had made a mistake in ducking into the mesquite. Had he simply kept going, he might have kept enough distance between himself and Colfax to be safe. He might have made it to a spot where he would have had the advantage rather than his pursuer. Another rifle shot rang out, and it was followed by a long, low rumble.

"The storm's acoming," he said out loud.

As Colfax cranked another shell into the chamber of the Winchester, he felt a sudden drop in temperature and saw a massive shadow move across the ground to encompass him. He looked up into the sky to see a blanket of dark clouds moving rapidly overhead.

"That's a relief," he said. He leveled the rifle once again across the saddle and fired another shot. A large drop of water splattered on the saddle horn.

"Gonna rain," he said, and he looked up into the sky. Another lone drop thunked into his right eye.

"Goddamn."

He ducked his head and rubbed his eye. Then he unrolled a slicker from behind his saddle and pulled it on. The raindrops were hard and heavy, and they were few and far between. The air was suddenly downright chilly. Colfax felt a sudden desperation. He fired three more rapid shots into the thicket. He hadn't quite worked his way into the center of the trees, and it seemed urgent that he get this job done. He looked at the sky, and another drop slapped him on the cheek. He took a new bead on the thicket and pulled the trigger only to discover that he had neglected to work the lever after his last shot. He cranked it, aimed again, and pulled. The rifle was empty.

"Goddamn it to hell," he said, reaching deep into his pocket for shells with which to reload. Then a loud clap of thunder caused the earth to vibrate beneath his feet. The roan squealed and vaulted. Colfax dropped shells and rifle in his haste to grab the roan before it stampeded in its fright, and someone upstairs overturned a very large bucket of water all at once. The roan stamped and reared. Colfax clung to the reins in desperation and fought to get into the saddle. Rain came in torrents and slashed at his face. He could see nothing beyond the roan.

"Whoa. Whoa," he shouted. "Damn you, stand still."

He managed to get a foot into a stirrup and swing into the saddle. Then horse and rider spun a few times in utter confusion. Colfax strained his eyes through the sheets of falling water until he thought he had located the mesquite thicket. Having regained a sense of direction, he cruelly dug his silver spurs into the ribs of the big roan and raced toward the thicket. It was the only place to go.

Huddled beneath mesquite branches, Luton wasn't dry, but he was somewhat protected from the driving rain. A sense of duty caused him to keep straining watchful eyes out toward the open landscape, but he knew that he couldn't see past the length of his arm in any direction. The sound of the rain was deafening. Though he couldn't see or hear Colfax, he was certain that the man was headed for the thicket. There was no other place for him to go, and the downpour was a perfect opportunity for him to get into the thicket undetected. *Yes,* thought Luton, *he's in here now somewhere. He's in here with me.*

Colfax was practically into the thicket before he saw clearly how close he was, and he rushed pell-mell into the tight brush, causing his roan to scream and buck when he felt his face slashed by thorny branches. Colfax almost lost his seat. He fought to regain control of the big horse as he dismounted. He pulled the animal a little ways farther into the stubby trees and quickly lashed the reins around a narrow trunk. He pulled the slicker up tight around his neck and under the brim of his Montana peak hat. He tried to huddle back into a tree, but the long thorns stabbed him through the layers of clothing and drove him away again. The roan finally decided that the mesquites gave him a reasonable amount of security, and he settled down. Colfax pulled his slicker more tightly around him and crawled underneath the horse's belly. He thought about the Winchester up on the top of the rise in the mud and rain, and he felt like a damn fool. At least his Colt was safe and dry underneath the slicker.

He tried to take his mind off the rain and chill in an effort to stop his own shivering. He put his mind back on the business at hand. His prey was right in these same trees with him. Perhaps only a few feet away. He had lost his rifle, but on reflection, he realized that it really didn't matter much. Riding into the thicket as he had done, he had given up the advantage the rifle had provided him with anyway. He slid a hand down his side and felt the Colt underneath the slicker to reassure himself. Yes. In here the six-gun was all that was needed. In fact, it was best. The brush was too tight to allow for maneuvering a rifle around. But he had given up the advantage in another and much more fundamental sense. He realized, sitting there beneath the belly of his horse, shivering in the driving rain, that he and his quarry were in exactly the same position now. Each knew the other was somewhere in the thicket. Each would try to find the other first. The distinction between hunter and hunted no longer existed, and Colfax felt a cold chill run through to his bones, and he realized that it had not been caused solely by the driving Texas rain.

It was no more than an hour before the rain stopped as abruptly as it had started. Colfax was instantly alert. He let the slicker slide off his back and down into the mud. Slowly he withdrew his Colt from his holster high on his waist and slightly to the right side, and he peered through the thick brush carefully from left to right. He could detect nothing. He eased himself up to his feet but remained in a low crouch, and he turned around slowly to look in the other direction. The thicket seemed much more extensive from inside than it had from out. He saw no sign of his prey. He tried to calculate his approximate position in the thicket compared to where he had sent his last rifle shot. Figuring that if any of his shots had come close to Luton, the marshal would have made some sign, he decided that he knew which way to look, and he began slithering his way through the brush.

In the calm after the storm, Bluff Luton sat and listened intently. The silence bothered him. He slipped off his yellow slicker and let it fall, then worked his way quickly and quietly to the edge of the thicket. He could see no sign of the man or the horse up the rise. He stepped slowly out into the open. As he pulled his boot out of the mud with each step, he thought that the suck could be heard for miles. He looked up and down the edge of the thicket and saw nothing, but he felt certain that Colfax was in there somewhere. He pulled out his Starr, and he heard a nicker off to his left. He turned and pointed toward the sound with the barrel of the Starr, and he caught a glimpse of the head of the big roan as it nodded once up above the tops of the scrawny mesquites. Colfax was probably no longer with the horse, thought Luton. He was probably working his way through the brush.

Luton sneaked his way back through the thicket to his own horse. He loosened the reins and led the animal the nearest way to the edge of the thicket, headed him out, and slapped him soundly on the rump, sending him running hard for the rise. Luton watched the brush. His horse wasn't halfway up the slope when the figure of Oliver Colfax, attracted by the sound of the running horse, popped up in the brush, his Colt pointed in the direction of the fleeing animal. Luton shouted and fired almost at the same time.

"Cole," he said. His shot ripped the wet, sagging brim of Colfax's Montana peak hat. As quickly as he fired, Luton dropped to the mud. Colfax fired back through the brush in Luton's direction, as Luton scooted back into the thicket and off to his right through the brush.

"Cole," he shouted. "Cole."

"I hear you."

"Cole, what's this all about?"

"It's time, Sarge," said Colfax. "I said I'd let you know."

"Cole, the Jessups are dead. Ain't no one to pay you. I don't want to kill you. Go back to your horse and ride out of here. I won't fire."

He wouldn't either, Colfax thought. *Be just like him to let me ride off from here. Damn.* He pointed his Colt in the direction of Luton's voice.

"I got to see this thing through," he shouted, and he pulled the trigger. The bullet splattered into the mud a few feet away from Luton. Luton decided then that Cole had had his chance. He wouldn't say anything more. It would be a fight to the finish. He scooted generally toward Colfax but, once again, sidling off to the right. That way, he thought, he might be able to come up on Cole from the side and surprise him. After oozing his way through the muck for several long minutes, Luton spotted Cole through the tangled branches. He squished himself a little closer before pointing the Starr and calling out.

"Don't move," he said, "or I'll kill you for sure."

Colfax sat still. He turned his head very slowly, just enough to glance out of the corner of his eye in the direction of the voice. He saw Luton's big Starr aimed dead at him.

"It looks like you got me," he said. "I wouldn't have believed it."

"Pitch your pistol," said Luton, standing up and starting to move toward Colfax. Colfax started to do as he had been told, but before he made the toss, Luton stepped on a slick, flat stone which had been hidden from sight by a thin layer of slimy clay from the rain. His foot shot forward, throwing him on his back in the mud, and his Starr flew from his hand off into the brush behind him. Colfax, reacting too quickly, swung his gun hand toward Luton and right into a three-inch mesquite thorn which buried itself in his wrist. He screamed in pain and surprise as his fingers straightened, causing him to drop his Colt into the mud. Luton scrambled to his feet and dove at Colfax, catching him around the shoulders. Both men splashed into the mud. But Colfax was quick, and he was stronger than Luton. He wrestled himself up on top, pinning Luton's arms down with his knees and pushing his hands into Luton's face. Luton could feel the soft mud running into his ears. He kicked and wriggled in an attempt to get himself out from under Colfax's bulk. Colfax, still holding Luton's face down with one hand, raised the other high in the air and made a fist which he brought down hard at Luton's head. Luton just managed to jerk his head aside enough to receive only a stinging, glancing blow to the side of the head, and Colfax was thrown off balance enough for Luton to wrench an arm loose. He reached across in front of Colfax and grabbed a low branch on the nearest mesquite and dragged it across Colfax's throat, the thorns slashing through flesh. Colfax growled in pain and rage and reached for the branch, but Luton quickly wrapped it around the big man's neck. Both of Cole's hands went for his neck, and he pushed himself upward with his powerful legs, tearing himself loose of the branch, but at the same time causing it to rip again in the opposite direction. Blood ran freely from several gashes around his neck. Luton tried to scramble to his feet, but Colfax gave him a vicious kick in the ribs that sent him sprawling back into the mud. Looking down, Colfax quickly located his fallen Colt, and he bent and picked it up out of the mud. Luton got to his hands and knees, but before he could stand, he looked up and found himself staring into the barrel of the Colt. It's over, he thought.

Colfax pulled back the hammer. He moved the barrel a few inches and pulled the trigger, firing into the mud to Luton's left.

"It's done," he said.

Chapter Twenty

Sergeant Bluff Luton stood under a large leafless shade tree and back in some bushes. It was snowing, but the tree gave him some shelter. His blanket roll was on the ground at his feet. He wore the yellow slicker over his black suit. His Starr revolver was strapped on under the suit coat. He was a little conspicuous. He was obviously a westerner, but aside from that he hadn't called too much attention to himself. It hadn't been difficult locating the home of George Fisher. Fisher was a prominent businessman in Boston. Just a couple of questions had led him to Fisher's place of business, and he had followed the man home. He had not been seen. It had been snowing when Luton got off the train at the Boston depot, and the snow had not let up. Luton had hopped a cab and followed Fisher's cab home when Fisher had left his office. At the Fisher house, Luton had paid his cabby and stepped out again into the snow. Fisher had gone inside while Luton stood in the snow and watched the two cabbies whip up their horses and drive off. He had walked in a direction away from Fisher's house, in case anyone had been watching, and when the cabs were out of sight, he had ducked quickly into the bushes and under the big tree. He had been watching the house for an hour.

He couldn't be sure, but he thought that Fisher was probably at home alone. He decided that he had waited long enough. He would chance it. He stepped out of the bushes, out from under the protection of the shade tree, and hurried across the street and down to the big Fisher house. He went up to the front door and pounded on it with his fist. Impatiently, he pounded again. As the door started to open from the inside, Luton shoved against it heavily, knocking George Fisher backward into the living room.

"Hey. What the hell . . . ?"

Fisher stopped his question when he saw the Starr in Luton's hand.

"Shut up," said Luton. "You're George Fisher?"

"Yeah. Who're you?"

"Never mind who I am. Is anyone else in the house?"

"No. Just me. What do you want?"

Luton thumbed back the hammer on the Starr. It was a double-action revolver and didn't need the thumbing back, but the motion and the sound it made was calculated to have an effect on Fisher. It worked. Fisher put his hands up over his head quickly.

"Don't shoot," he said. "Don't shoot. Just tell me what you want."

Luton walked up close to Fisher and drove his left fist into Fisher's midsection. Fisher doubled over with a groan. Then Luton slapped him across the side of the face with the revolver. Fisher reeled to one side and sank to his knees. Blood ran down the side of his face and dripped onto his expensive carpet. He put a hand up to feel the gash in his face.

"Stand up," said Luton.

Fisher hesitated, and Luton kicked him across the back, knocking him flat on his face. Fisher screamed as he sprawled on the carpet.

"Get up," said Luton.

"All right. All right," said Fisher, staggering to his feet. "Tell me what you want. Please."

Luton looked at the rich man standing there before him.

He glanced at the surroundings, plush, luxurious, but, Luton thought, garish and tasteless. He noticed the expensive shirt with fresh bloodstains. Then he took note of the man himself, a big, healthy-appearing man, not at all bad looking. Why did a man like this need to mistreat a woman? Luton thought of Emily and little Matthew. Then he swung his left again, smashing his fist into the side of Fisher's jaw. Fisher was thrown sideways and fell heavily across a fancy but flimsy coffee table which stood before an over-stuffed couch. The legs of the table gave way, and Fisher landed on the floor, broken table beneath him. Luton moved after him and pulled him to his feet by his shirtfront. Then he shoved him backward onto the couch. He still held the Starr aimed at Fisher's chest.

"Now, Mr. Fisher," he said, "do I have your attention?"

Fisher gasped for breath.

"Do I have your attention, I asked you."

"Yes. Yes," said Fisher.

Luton reached with his left hand into the pocket of his suit coat and pulled out the little derringer he had gotten from Matthew. He held it up in front of him.

"Do you see this?" he said.

"Yes."

"Do you recognize it?"

"No," said Fisher. "It's a little gun."

"I took it away from a man named Ryan," said Luton. "You know Ryan?"

"Ryan?" said Fisher. "Yeah, I know."

Luton threw the derringer hard into Fisher's stomach. Fisher doubled over with a groan.

"I want you to give that back to Mr. Ryan. Will you do that for me?"

"Yes. Yes."

"Do I still have your attention?"

"Yes."

"Because I want you to listen good," said Luton. "Listen real good. Your life depends on it. You sent that man after a lady. A lady you were once fortunate enough to call your wife. You no longer have any claim on that lady, nor on her child. Do you understand me?''

"Yeah. Yeah, but why . . . ?''

"Shut up. Just listen to me. You don't know me. You don't know my name. You don't know where I come from or anything about me. But I'm going to tell you one thing, and you can believe it. Are you listening?''

"Yes.''

"If anything ever happens to either that lady or her boy, I won't ask how it happened. I won't slow down to find out whether or not you had anything to do with it. I'll come back here and kill you. You got that?''

"Yes.''

"Now come with me.''

"Where?'' said Fisher.

Luton gestured toward the front door with his Starr.

"Move,'' he said.

Fisher staggered to the door, and Luton made him go outside and across the street in the snow, back to the bushes and the shade tree he had lurked by earlier.

"Now take off your clothes,'' said Luton.

"What?''

"You heard me. Just do it.''

Fisher stood undecided, hesitating.

"Fisher,'' said Luton, "I could kill you now and save myself a lot of trouble.''

Fisher undressed and stood shivering in the snow. Luton picked up the clothes and walked away. A few blocks down the street, he tossed them aside. It would take Fisher awhile to get himself back into his house without being seen naked on the street. Then it would take him some time to get dressed again and get to the police, if that was his intention. By then Luton would be back at the depot. The train west would leave soon, and then Fisher would have no idea who to send anyone after. Luton didn't think that Fisher would do anything, though. The man was a coward. Emily and Matt would be all right in Texas, and Luton would take one last, long train ride back to his quiet job, where he would start growing soft again right away, and that was just fine with him. Yes, he was convinced that he and Emily and Matt had heard the last of George Fisher.

About the Author

ROBERT J. CONLEY is a writer, scholar, editor, poet, and part Cherokee. His recent books include *Back to Malachi* and *The Saga of Henry Starr*. He is a professor of English at Morningside College in Sioux City, Iowa.